# NORSE MYTHS

## VIKING LEGENDS OF HEROES AND GODS

# NORSE MYTHS

## VIKING LEGENDS OF HEROES AND GODS

MARTIN J. DOUGHERTY

**amber**
BOOKS

Published by
Amber Books Ltd
74–77 White Lion Street
London
N1 9PF
United Kingdom
www.amberbooks.co.uk
Appstore: itunes.com/apps/amberbooksltd
Facebook: www.facebook.com/amberbooks
Twitter: @amberbooks

ISBN: 978-1-78274-332-3

Project Editor: Michael Spilling
Designer: Zoe Mellors
Picture Research: Terry Forshaw

Printed in China

# CONTENTS

# THE NORSEMEN

The stories of Thor, Odin and Loki are at least vaguely familiar to most of us. Many people can recall – often without being able to say exactly where they heard the story – that the Norse gods fought against giants and were ultimately betrayed by Loki the trickster. The end of the world and the death of the gods in a grim battle called Ragnarok has also found its way into popular culture.

People who would never consider studying mythology may know a surprising amount about the religion of the Norse people, often without realizing they do. One reason for this is the profound influence that Norse mythology has had upon other cultures, causing the legends to filter through to today, not only in the histories of the Norse people themselves, but from other sources, too. Ideas 'borrowed' from Norse mythology are frequently found in modern fantasy and science fiction – such as elves, dwarfs and undead warriors rising from an unquiet grave, for example.

OPPOSITE: Dating from the twelfth century, long after the 'Viking Age', this tapestry depicts Odin, Freya and Thor. Much of our knowledge of the Norse mythos comes from such later sources; little was recorded at the time.

In some cases, the use of Norse characters in modern stories is deliberate. In *Marvel's* graphic novels and movies, Thor and his fellow gods are an advanced race whose science gives them god-like powers, but they are essentially the same people as in the original myths. In David Drake's *Northworld* series of novels, the lead characters are parallels of the Norse gods – Commander North himself lost an eye in return for knowledge of the future, as did Odin the Allfather. This use of mythical characters is quite deliberate on the part of the author.

Other influences may be less obvious, and, indeed, the creator might not be aware of the process by which he or she ended up adding Norse concepts to a novel of modern fantasy or science fiction. Magical weaponry made by dwarfs is a common fantasy trope; few realize that it comes from Norse legend. Similarly, there are numerous 'Ragnarok Devices' and 'Ragnarok Operations' in science fiction; the meaning is obvious even to those who do not know anything about the original mythology.

BELOW: **The modern fascination with the Norsemen has resulted in detailed reconstruction of their homes and way of life, such as here at L'Anse aux Meadows, Newfoundland.**

There are many reasons why Norse characters and stories exert such a powerful influence whereas other mythologies do not. For one thing, these are interesting characters whose adventures make a great story. Other mythologies have equally fascinating concepts, but are less well known. They require more explanation and will not necessarily grab the audience's attention in the same way. A familiar story rings true: a familiar character is easy to identify with. So the mythology of the Norsemen continues to inspire and entertain us today, and one reason for that is the Norsemen themselves.

## The Norsemen

Often (rather inaccurately) referred to as 'Vikings', the Norse people inhabited Scandinavia – modern Denmark, Norway and Sweden as well as parts of Finland – and spread out into other regions. In what is now Russia they became known as 'the Rus', who heavily influenced the development of that country. Their settlements in Normandy, France, were recognized by the King of the Franks and became a European duchy from which the present monarchy of the United Kingdom is derived. William the Conqueror was Duke of Normandy, something different from a Norse war-leader, but his lineage and traditions originated in the Norse world.

THE NEWFOUNDLAND AND GREENLAND NORSE COLONIES ARE LONG GONE, BUT ICELAND PROSPERED AND BECAME A MODERN NATION.

The Norsemen also settled in Iceland, Greenland and even a very small part of North America (Newfoundland) – although the latter was extremely short-lived. These Newfoundland and Greenland colonies are long gone, but Iceland prospered and became a modern nation. It was there that many of the heroic sagas of the Norse people were finally written down, and it is from Icelandic tradition that we derive much of what we know about the Norsemen and their gods.

The term 'Viking', often applied to Norsemen in general, in fact referred to someone who was involved in an expedition, or 'Vik'. An expedition was defined as a journey where it was necessary to take turns at the oars of a ship; short trips where the

vessel was rowed directly to the destination in one shift at the oars did not qualify for the term. More generally, an expedition was considered to mean any long journey on land or sea, and anyone undertaking one was a Viking – but only until he returned home.

The most famous Norse 'expeditions' were, of course, their increasingly destructive raids along the coasts of Europe, but they were equally willing to trade. Some expeditions were a bit of both, depending on the wealth of the places visited and how well guarded they appeared to be. These raiding and trade expeditions took Norsemen around the coasts of Europe and into the Mediterranean, and, of course, some settled in lands they found pleasing. The British Isles and the coasts of northern Europe and Iceland were extensively settled, as well as areas inland of the Baltic Sea.

Trade expeditions (and raids) got as far as the Arab world, and pushed some way up the Silk Road. There have been somewhat fanciful attempts to connect what appears to be runic graffiti in Southeast Asia with a 'Viking' expedition along the trade routes of the Silk Road to China, then down the Yangtze River and along the Pacific Coast. There are even claims that Norsemen reached Australia, but these do not come from credible sources. Likewise, the settlement of North America has been greatly exaggerated by some, with numerous fake artefacts 'proving' that there were Norse settlements in the American interior when it is almost certain that there were not.

Leaving aside the wilder claims about where the Norsemen went and what they did, it is certainly true that they visited many places and left an impression – both good and bad. The Byzantine emperors maintained an elite unit called the Varangian Guard that was initially recruited from the warriors of the Rus, who were themselves relocated Norsemen. The Varangian Guard later took recruits from much of northern Europe, although these often came from Norse-influenced regions.

BELOW: Using the great rivers of Europe and Russia as highways, the Norsemen reached the Middle East where they interacted with Arab traders. This created a link to the Silk Road reaching all the way to China.

Wherever the Norsemen raided, legends sprang up about them. Where they settled, they brought their own myths and stories, and these endured long after the adoption of Christianity. Indeed, for a time many Norsemen were happy to accept both Christianity and their older gods side-by-side. Over time, however, the Norse gods faded into myth, although their cultural influence was still felt.

## THE MERGING OF MYTH AND REALITY

The legendary 'dragon ships' of the Norsemen are an example of how fact and fiction have become distorted. The term 'dragon ship' has been used for many years to describe the longships used for raids and trading expeditions. These ships did indeed have a carved prow in the shape of a fearsome creature, but no clear evidence of a dragon has ever been found. Serpents, horses and all manner of other designs have been identified by archaeologists, and of course it is possible that dragon designs were popular, but none have survived.

The term 'dragon ship' is of obscure origins. Some historical sources seem to imply a connection between the Norse ships and dragons, possibly of a more fanciful nature than a description of the carved prow. It could be that the chroniclers recorded a garbled version of eyewitness accounts – after all, as a vessel full of bloodthirsty Norsemen approaches, the average villager could be forgiven for failing to note that the prow is carved as a serpent rather than a dragon! Or it might be the result of hyperbole or bardic speech. The Skalds, who were part historian, part bard and part data-retrieval system, used phrases known as 'Kennings' in their poetry. Kennings could be quite simple, such as 'sea-steed' for ship, or subtle and complex. A term like 'wave-dragon' could be taken to mean a ship with a dragon-carved prow or a boatload of rapacious Vikings descending to bring chaos upon their victims.

LEFT: **The carved prows of Norse ships were undoubtedly a source of great pride and gave the vessel its own identity – something that might be important to men who had to cross many miles of open sea in it.**

The Norsemen were a hardy folk from a land that could often be challenging. They were willing to undertake long voyages in open vessels, and even invented ways of navigating on the ocean. They were certainly a brave people, but although they were entirely willing to use violence when needed, there were actually very few professional warriors in Norse culture. Most 'Vikings' went back to their farms or trades after an expedition and many never ventured forth at all. However, they were raised on tales of battling gods and they respected courage, skill at arms and similar martial values. The Norsemen were thus part-time warriors-at-need – albeit enthusiastic ones – rather than a race of professional fighting-men.

Norse traders and settlers carried with them their stories and myths, and these inevitably became distorted over time as well as merging with those of other cultures. As a result there may be numerous variants of a tale, or distorted versions that in some cases have drifted so far from the original as to be almost unrecognizable except in the most general of terms. Similarly, the real Norsemen have become confused with fictional versions or with their own myths, to the point where an extremely distorted image has emerged.

Norse mythology is also distorted, from our perspective, by the fact that there was little writing in the so-called 'Viking Age'. Runes were used, but important information was enshrined in the writing of the Skalds, the Norse poets who recorded and celebrated heroic deeds, and kept alive by recitation and the training of new Skalds. The sagas were not written down until long after the end of the 'Viking Age', and were further distorted by comparison to other mythologies.

Most of what we know about the Norse mythology has been inferred from fragmented and sometimes contradictory references in the Poetic and Prose Eddas. These are traditional Norse tales written down years later, mostly in Iceland, and in many cases the mythology contained in them is presented as part of the story of a mortal hero.

There is no single 'holy book' that can be used as a self-contained reference, and no guarantee that any given piece of information is completely correct.

The Icelandic scholar Snorri Sturluson, from whose work most of the commonly accepted versions of the Norse tales are derived, was writing in the period 1200–1240 AD, long after the end of the 'Viking Age', and more importantly, long after Christianity had supplanted the old Norse religion. In places he seems to have invented details to 'tidy up' the Norse pantheon, creating relationships between gods and giants to give other gods named parents even though there seems to be no evidence for such a relationship in the original versions.

Sturluson also seems to impose Christian values on some Norse concepts; his representation of death and the afterlife seems particularly influenced by the Christian idea of heaven and an underground hell.

It is inevitable that chroniclers from other cultures would make comparisons to help them understand the Norse gods. However, this can be confusing – Thor is Thor, not the Roman god Mars with added lightning powers! Comparisons of this sort are helpful in a very basic way, but overall can serve to confuse the issue, creating a sort of pan-European monomythology that never existed.

ABOVE: **A fourteenth-century manuscript of the Poetic Edda, which was originally compiled by Snorri Sturluson from traditional Norse poems. Distortion is perhaps inevitable given the time between the replacement of the Norse religion by Christianity and the recording of its tales.**

## Misconceptions

Our perception of the Norse people and their gods was further distorted by the Victorian revival of interest in the field. In the Victorian era there was a great deal of interest in the Classical period (Ancient Greece and Rome) and a number of false comparisons were made between these cultures and those of the Norsemen. Norse warriors gained winged helmets, for which there is no archaeological evidence, in romantic Victorian depictions. They also tended to be represented as wearing anachronistic clothing and armour.

THE IMAGE OF NORSEMEN AS WANTON DESTROYERS COMES MAINLY FROM THEIR VICTIMS.

The Victorian image of the Norsemen was of 'noble savages', and some other aspects of their mythology were also sanitized. For example, the Valkyries who bore fallen warriors to Valhol (the word Valhalla is another distortion from the same era) were originally hags associated with carrion beasts, but in later depictions they are changed into beautiful warrior-maidens. The angels of Christianity received a similar treatment – originally they were terrible in countenance, with three heads and six wings, and inspired great fear. Modern depictions of serene and beautiful angels are much more pleasant to look at; the same goes for modern Valkyries.

Another common image of the Norsemen is, of course, as violent and primitive savages. This version of the 'Vikings' depicted them as psychopaths who wore horned helmets and drank out of skulls. Again, there is no evidence for horns on Norse helmets, which is hardly surprising since they would be a huge liability in battle and likely to become tangled in the ropes and stays of a ship. The image of Norsemen as wanton destroyers comes mainly from their victims, some of whom were Christians who went on to write histories of how the Norsemen with their pagan gods came to the great houses of Christianity and plundered them. They did not have much reason to try for a fair and balanced viewpoint.

Thus today's image of the Norsemen themselves is severely distorted, and our understanding of their religion equally so. Yet, to some extent at least, it is through this very distortion that the Norse mythos has become so prevalent. It has spread out across Europe and the wider world to the point where a thousand years after the Norse gods ceased to be widely worshipped they are still exerting a strong cultural influence.

BELOW: Even before the Iron Age reached Scandinavia the Norsemen were capable of making high-quality weapons and other metal objects. This well-made and decorated bronze spearhead would have been as effective as most iron ones, if less durable.

# Origins of the Norsemen

In very general terms, the people who would become the Norsemen may have entered Scandinavia between 8000–4000BC, as the region warmed up after the end of the Ice Age. The early inhabitants would have been semi-nomadic hunters who gradually settled into a static lifestyle as farmers and herders. The Bronze Age began around 2000–1500 BC in Scandinavia; better tools made of metal allowed more efficient farming and craftsmanship, enabling the region to support a larger population than previously.

The widespread use of iron reached Scandinavia around 500 BC, again enabling the creation of better tools and weapons. Iron was readily available in most of the region, making iron-working preferable to bronze not only for the better quality and durability of tools but also because there was no longer a need to trade for the constituents of bronze.

It is known that the Scandinavian people of this time had contact with other Germanic peoples in northern Europe, and through them with the Roman Empire. Scandinavian culture was influenced – at least a little – by the proto-Celtic and, later, Celtic cultures of Europe and also by Roman society. Some Roman sources mention the names of Scandinavian places, although the accuracy of these accounts is debatable.

Sea-borne raiding and trade was common in Scandinavia at this time, although the vessels in use were not capable of long voyages or crossing open seas. Evidence from burial sites suggests that Scandinavia was prosperous, but also that conflict was common, probably on a small scale. Coastal raids were common enough that hillforts and other fortifications were built, but there is little evidence of large-scale warfare. This is more than likely due to the lack of large and organized states.

Around 400 AD, the Huns began pushing into Europe and caused enormous upheaval. This did not directly affect Scandinavia in a major way; there was no Hunnic invasion of that region. However, in the years that followed many of the Germanic peoples were displaced and began to wander generally eastwards seeking new homelands. This, along with a possible influx of Slavic and Finnish peoples driven north into

Scandinavia, may have resulted in some major social changes.

Originally, Scandinavia shared a language with the Germanic peoples in mainland Europe, but between 550–750 AD the language changed rapidly to create the *dönsk tunga*, or 'Danish Tongue'. The *dönsk tunga* was spoken throughout Scandinavia and the regions settled by Norsemen, but evolved into local dialects that eventually drifted apart, such that eastern areas (for example, Sweden and Denmark) spoke almost a different language to the settlers in Iceland or Ireland.

While the rest of Europe was in the throes of the *Völkerwanderung*, or Migration Period, Scandinavia was stable with only low-level conflict. The upheaval that accompanied the migrations resulted in new nations appearing, often with characteristics derived from several component tribes. This ensured that some elements of the proto-Scandinavian culture were widely disseminated, but by 800 AD the emergent nations of Europe were very different from their Scandinavian equivalents that had not been flung into the cultural blender along with the others.

This era is known as the Vendel Period, after a major archaeological find from the time. It saw the emergence of a proto-Norse culture whose upper echelons were rich enough to import horses from the emerging kingdom of the Franks. Some of the legends and sagas from this era refer to princes and highborn warriors fighting on horseback, although foot combat was the norm.

Much of what we know of this era comes from archaeological finds such as that at Vendel. These included great riches and extremely high-quality craftsman-made items as well as goods that can only have been imported. During this period, shipbuilding technology advanced to the point where it was possible to trade in

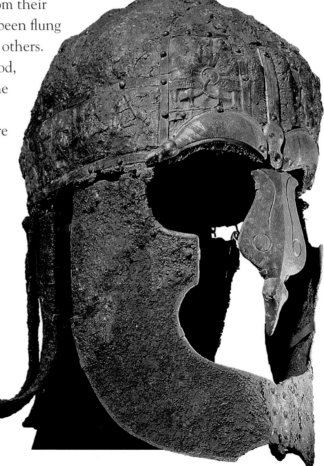

BELOW: This helmet from the Vendel period, which immediately preceded the 'Viking Age', is better suited to actual combat than the winged monstrosities of modern depiction. The cheek-pieces might indicate a Roman influence.

RIGHT: **The popular image of Viking raiders pillaging the holy places of Europe began with a raid on Lindisfarne in 793 AD. The Norsemen were not making war on God, however. The motivation was simply profit.**

the British Isles and to settle the Orkneys. Lengthy expeditions became possible, bringing about what is normally called the Viking Age. This is normally defined as beginning in 793 AD with the first large-scale 'Viking' raid on Lindisfarne, a tidal island on the northeast coast of England. However, Scandinavian ships had been making expeditions to Britain for at least a few years previously. By the common definition of the term, the crews of these ships were Vikings.

The Viking Age was characterized by raids of increasing size. At first, one or two ships would attack a remote settlement or poorly defended town. Later, fleets comprising hundreds of ships launched large-scale campaigns, and Norse armies fought for control of large areas of land. The 'Viking Age' is considered to end in 1066, at the Battle of Hastings. By then, there were 'Viking kingdoms' in various areas, notably around York in England as well as in Scandinavia. One of them had evolved into a European duchy, and it was the victory of this state in the three-way fight for England that brought the 'Viking Age' to an end. By this point, Christianity had displaced the old Norse religion and the Norsemen themselves had undergone huge social changes. Yet, although their time had passed, the Norsemen of old continued to exert an influence on European culture that was every bit as important as that of Ancient Greece or Rome.

## Runes

Runes were symbols that conveyed a meaning, but were not quite the same thing as letters or pictograms. They could spell out words, but might also be used to convey a meaning that went beyond spelling and grammar. Runes could, in many cases, function as letters, representations of sounds or word fragments, and also as pictograms encompassing an idea. Which way a rune was interpreted depended on context. This can make modern translation difficult, not least because the rules for interpreting runes varied from time to time and place to place even when they were in common use.

RUNES COULD SPELL OUT WORDS, BUT COULD ALSO REPRESENT IDEAS, SOUNDS OR WORD FRAGMENTS.

Systems of runes are often called alphabets or runic alphabets, but they can also be thought of as a character set that can have multiple meanings. The term used for a set of Germanic runes is Futhark, a word derived from the first six runes in the same way as 'alphabet' is derived from the first two symbols of the Greek alphabet. The Ogham writing used by the ancient Celts probably originated around the first century AD and consists of straight lines that are easy to carve on wood, stone or bone. It was an alphabetical system used to write down the languages of the time, and is contemporary with, but separate from, the Germanic Futharks.

The earliest known Futhark, the Elder Futhark, first appeared around the first century AD and was fully developed by 400 AD or so. Around 750AD, the beginning of the 'Viking Age', the Elder Futhark was supplanted by the Younger Futhark, which had 16 runes instead of 24. In Anglo-Saxon lands, the Anglo-Saxon

Futhorc was used, which had 38 characters. The Anglo-Saxon Futhorc and the Elder Futhark were both used in Europe and were eventually amalgamated by some users.

Modern scholars generally believe that runic writing was introduced to the Germanic peoples of northern Europe from the Mediterranean, and that early runes may have been derived from the Italic language that preceded Latin. However, the Norsemen had a much more dramatic tale of how they gained the use of runes. Seeking wisdom, the god Odin spent nine nights hanging from a tree -- which was probably Yggdrasil, the World Tree – impaled on his own spear. During his ordeal, he gazed into the Well of Urd, which reflected the past, and learned much before seizing the runes and gaining their power.

Thus the Norsemen viewed the runes as more than a means of writing messages. They were a source of power and a gift from Odin the Allfather, and could be used to communicate not only with people but also with beings and forces beyond the mortal realm. In some ways, the runes could be considered as a means of communicating with the universe itself, and could affect reality if used correctly. The Norse sagas feature heroes who could do magic by inscribing the right runes on a pole or a medium such as a piece of bone, and who knew enough to recognize the effects of runic magic practiced by others.

It has been suggested that runes were used in divination of the future or seeing what is hidden, although there is very little evidence that this might have been the case. The concept of runic divination has found its way into modern fantasy and is widely accepted as having a historical basis, but it may be that the Norsemen did not in fact practice divination using the runes.

Observers from outside the Norse world recorded divinations by various means, but often the text is unclear as to whether runes were used or some other means. This has not stopped various more recent proponents from putting forward systems of divination using the runes and claiming (with

BELOW: The runes were shaped so as to be easy to carve into stone, with angular shapes and no curves. This imaginative inscription, with most of its runes inside a serpent, was found near Stockholm, Sweden.

or without much evidence) that their method is a traditional Norse system. Various forms of 'Germanic Mysticism' have appeared over the years, many of which have aspects in common with tarot reading. Some, however, contend that the runes have more direct powers than divination.

There are clear references in the traditional tales of runes being used for magical purposes. Rune spells could be used to promote healing or to bring victory in battle, to improve eloquence or to protect a ship from the vagaries of wind and wave. The Poetic and Prose Eddas refer to specific instances where characters use runic magic, and at one point a Valkyrie catalogues the magical effects possible using the runes. Since the runes could be used to reshape reality, it may be that they were not well suited to divination, as this is intended to reveal truths and futures already set, whereas rune magic could alter that future.

## Norse Mythology and Other Cultures

There are many parallels between Norse mythology and that of other cultures. Some of these may have come about retroactively, as cultures melded or scholars from one society tried to explain another's religion in familiar terms. Myths and even gods might be 'borrowed' from one pantheon and added to another through cultural pollution. Equally, it is possible that two mythologies might arise completely separately yet look surprisingly similar.

In any pantheon there are certain roles that tend to be – or indeed need to be – filled. The gods must have a leader, and his rule will likely be challenged by someone within his circle of fellows. There will be antagonists of some kind, and gods who fulfil certain roles that parallel those of people in the ancient world. Thus some kind of fertility or love deity is necessary along with a warrior, a scholar and gods representing other important roles. The Norse pantheon has all of these, but the way these gods fulfil their roles can be highly complex.

In common with Roman and Ancient Greek religion, the gods of Norse mythology overthrew their predecessors to become pre-eminent. In Norse mythology these beings are the Jotnar (singular Jotunn), or Giants, but this word should not be taken

ABOVE: A poem ('Mary's Lament') written in runes. The original dates from the fourteenth century, a time when runic writing had been replaced by Latin script, at least for learned and holy men.

too literally as meaning 'big'. In fact, a better translation is 'Devourer'. Some of the Jotnar are depicted as huge, but others seem to be around the same size as other gods or even humans. What they are is important, powerful, god-like … but not gods. In this the Jotnar are similar to the Titans of Greek myth. Indeed, it is useful to equate the word 'Jotunn' to 'Titan' rather than 'Giant' to avoid confusion with various forms of monstrous and non-divine giants that appear in other mythologies and in fiction.

As in Greek mythology the Norse gods overthrew their titanic forebears and became rulers of the universe, but not without challenge. The Jotnar plot against the gods and will, at the end of the gods' time, march against them to mutual destruction. However, they are also at times taken as wives by the gods, although the Norse gods were not receptive to the idea that any of their goddesses could become a Jotunn's wife.

The Greek and Roman gods tended to be a lot more aloof than their Norse equivalents. Roman and especially Greek gods were prone to meddling in the affairs of individual humans, usually to their detriment. They seem to have fathered a considerable number of semi-divine children by human women, and then used those children as pawns in their schemes against the other gods or ruined the lives of these demigod-children through jealousy. In short, the Greek and Roman gods were not very good friends to humans.

The Norse gods had a different relationship with mortals. To the average Norse person, the gods were like distant family members, powerful, of course, but approachable by someone willing to speak his or her mind. Gods were not to be propitiated so much as bargained with, and it was not unknown for a Norseman to more or less threaten his gods. Aid might be demanded, or else the Norseman would have a major falling-out with his god. This was not disrespect so much as a different form of respect to that found in many religions. Gods were powerful, but the relationship between them and mortals was a two-way street and humans had a right to expect fair treatment – or at least to be angry with the gods for not giving it.

Similarly, Norse gods tended to be more complex than those of other pantheons. Odin, for example, was the wise leader of the gods that is a traditionally male role in ancient societies. He was also a powerful warrior – again, a traditionally male role. But Odin was also the master of magic, which was considered effeminate in Norse society. Spells were normally a matter for women or hag-like beings, and were beneath the pride of heroic and manly figures. Yet Odin, who as Allfather is surely the manliest of all the gods, practices magic.

Complex as the Norse gods may have been, with one exception they were not capricious. The gods had their own agenda and pursued it without regard to others if necessary. This caused conflict with other gods and at times upset their human worshippers, but there was always a reason – the gods of the Norse world did not toy with mortals for their amusement. Whereas the Greek and Roman gods at times amused themselves at mortals' expense, and could be wildly unpredictable, the Norse gods were constant and reliable. This was not always a good thing – making an enemy of someone who does not change is distinctly hazardous – but it did mean that a Norseman knew where he stood in relation to his gods.

The only god who changed in Norse religion was, predictably enough, the trickster Loki. At first he was capricious and rather difficult to have around, but he served a valuable purpose and sometimes was the only god who could deal with certain problems. His nature allowed him to use trickery that the other gods simply could not, and solved at least as many problems as it caused. However, Loki's pranks eventually turned nasty and led to savage punishment after he more or less murdered Baldr, most beloved of all the gods. This punishment in turn resulted in Loki becoming an implacable foe of the gods; it is he that led the Jotnar against them on

OPPOSITE: Carvings in wood and stone offer a tantalizing glimpse into the Norse mythos as recorded by the Norsemen themselves. Unfortunately, no simple guide to interpreting these carvings exists, and inferences have to be made using later sources.

## EXPLORING THE NORSE REALMS

As with many other mythologies, Norse religion had several 'worlds'. Most religions have a place of the dead, which may be subdivided into places where good, bad and indifferent people go, a place of the gods and a mortal realm, but the Norse religion was a lot more complex than this. There were several worlds all connected by Yggdrasil, the World-Tree, including realms of the gods and different groups of Jotnar, plus a mortal realm, several different places where the dead might go, and also realms belonging to Elves and Dwarfs, who were powerful beings in their own right.

the day of Ragnarok. However, Loki was mainly concerned with tricking other gods; even he had better things to do than messing mortals around.

There are close parallels between the Norse religion and that of the Anglo-Saxons, largely due to common origins. The Anglo-Saxons and other Germanic people were originally close neighbours of the Norsemen, and although they were displaced by turbulent events in Europe and later conquests, they worshipped the same gods. Linguistic differences and varying cultural influences resulted in the names of Anglo-Saxon deities

RIGHT: The Jotnar ('giants') of Norse mythology were not necessarily – as depicted here – particularly large. Many were no greater in stature than Thor, seen here in the foreground with a winged helm.

differing from their Norse counterparts, but they were essentially the same – the Anglo-Saxon Woden was Odin, his wife was Frige (Frigg) and their son Thunor was Thor.

Conversely, the Norse religion was very different from Christianity. The most obvious difference is the lack of a pantheon in Christianity – a single god fulfils all functions and the antagonist/enemy god is an angel who got above his station. There are still some parallels of course – Odin suffers on a tree, impaled by a spear, and sacrifices his eye to gain wisdom, whereas Christ redeems the world under similar circumstances. The Christian god tends not to venture around the world having adventures, although he was not above a wrestling match with the mortal Jacob.

Another key difference between the Christian religion and that of the Norse people was that while both predicted the End of Days in one form or another, valiant Norsemen were offered the chance to take part in this final battle. Those who survived would have a place in the renewed and wondrous world that came after. The next life, for some at least, was not the end of the journey, but a period of preparation for Ragnarok with the chance to win a place in the new world thereafter.

These differences did not prevent Norsemen from adopting Christianity, although many at first took the Christian god into their beliefs alongside all the others. Moulds have survived that allow the casting of a pendant that could be taken either as Christ's cross or Odin's hammer, depending upon preference. This is understandable – people who already acknowledge multiple gods are more likely to accept another one than those who follow a monotheistic religion. It is likely that early Christian Norsemen took a similar attitude to their new god as their old ones, shouting threats and curses at the sky when displeased by a lack of assistance. In time, however, Christian practices pushed out the older Norse ones until the old gods took on the aspect of folk heroes rather than deities.

## IDENTIFYING NORSE GODS

In Norse mythology there were two sets of gods – the Vanir, who personified love/fertility, and the Aesir, who represented war and martial virtues. The Anglo-Saxon versions were the Wen and the Ése, who likewise battle the Etin (i.e. the Jotnar). Much of the influence on modern fantasy comes by way of the Anglo-Saxon version of the Germanic/Norse mythos. The work of author J.R.R. Tolkien was so immensely influential that he is often considered the 'father of modern fantasy'. His influences included his own study of Anglo-Saxon heroic myths, notably the saga of Beowulf. It is mostly through Tolkien that modern fantasy gained its 'standard version' of elves, dwarfs and similar beings.

# CREATION AND COSMOLOGY

One of the fundamental questions asked by mortals is 'How did we get here?' Norse mythology provides answers to this question and many others, laying the foundations for the adventures of gods and humans.

The cosmology of the Norse mythos was more complex than many others, with several worlds all interconnected as part of a wider universe. Each of these worlds had its own characteristics and, in some cases, unique inhabitants.

## The Creation of the Universe

Before the world came into existence, there were two lands separated by an abyss. Muspelheim was a land of fire, Niflheim a land of ice and cold mist. Between them was the Ginnungagap, a void that was at once empty and charged with magic. The Ginnungagap contained the potential for all things, but was also the place that the world would collapse into when destroyed.

OPPOSITE: Norse mythology is full of mystical creatures, gods and powerful spirits. The three Norns tended the great tree Yggdrasil with water from the Well of Urd, giving them insight and power over the fate of mortals.

Muspelheim lay to the south of the Ginnungagap and was ruled over by a fire giant named Surt. It is not clear from the original sources when or where Surt came to be; he is simply noted as the lord of Muspelheim. In any case, the fires of Muspelheim flowed north in the form of lava and into the Ginnungagap.

In Niflheim to the north was Hvergelmir, source of all the cold waters in the cosmos. From there the Elivagar (ice waves) flowed south towards the Ginnungagap. These glaciers are described in the Prose Edda as being composed of 'yeasty venom'. When the creeping ice reached the Ginnungagap, the heat from Muspelheim caused it to melt, creating droplets that eventually formed a creature named Ymir.

Ymir is sometimes described as a hermaphrodite, although the term applies more in the mystical than physical sense. Ymir was certainly capable of bringing forth life without the assistance of another being; the sweat from Ymir's armpits formed into two Jotnar, or giants, and a third was formed by a mating of Ymir's legs or feet. These three Jotnar, two male and one female, were the first of the Hrimthursar, or Frost Giants.

BELOW: The primordial Jotunn, Ymir, was created by the meeting of ice and fire in the magically-charged Ginnungagap. He was the progenitor of the Jotnar and his body provided the basic material to make the world, though the actual creation was carried out by others.

LEFT: The magical cow Audhumbla provided food for Ymir and his offspring. She fed off the salt found in the ice that flowed from Niflheim and so revealed the first of the Aesir, Buri, whose offspring brought disaster to Ymir and Audhumbla.

The melting of ice from Niflheim also revealed a cow, named Audhumbla, which licked salt from the ice to feed herself and provided Ymir with milk. As she licked the ice, Audhumbla revealed another creature. This was Búri, and he was neither a Jotunn nor a cow, but the first of a tribe of gods named the Aesir. Búri had a son named Bor, who took a descendent of Ymir as his wife; this was the giantess Bestla.

The firstborn offspring of Bor and Bestla was named Odin. He was half Jotunn and half Aesir, and after him came his brothers Vili and Ve. Meanwhile, Ymir was continuing to produce more Jotnar, and this concerned Odin greatly – so greatly that he decided to kill Ymir and end the flow of Jotnar.

# THE CREATION OF MIDGARD

The gods made Midgard, which would be the home for humans, from Ymir's eyebrows or eyelashes. Midgard was unusual in the whole of the cosmos, in that it was the only one of the worlds that was wholly in the realm that could be perceived by mortals. All of the other worlds touched the mortal realm in some way, but were for the most part beyond the sight of mortal men. Midgard was protected from the giants and other threats by a fence built around it, separating it from the realms of the Jotnar. Some versions of the tale suggest that the fence was made from Ymir's eyebrows and are vague about what Midgard was made from; others seem to suggest that the whole land – presumably including the fence – was formed from Ymir's brows.

Waiting until Ymir was asleep, the three Aesir brothers attacked him. The battle was hard and resulted in a torrent of blood that drowned all but two of the Jotnar. These were Bergelmir and his wife; they survived by floating away in some kind of improvised boat. Exactly what form this vessel took depends on the version of the tale. It may be that Bergelmir and his wife constructed a canoe out of a hollowed-out tree trunk, while other versions of the tale refer to a chest or box used as a boat instead. By this means they escaped into Niflheim where they founded a new race of Frost Giants. The cow Audhumbla was also a casualty of the battle – she was swept over the edge into the abyss of Ginnungagap and was destroyed.

Odin and his brothers had successfully destroyed almost all of the Frost Jotnar, and more importantly their source, Ymir. From his body they fashioned the entire cosmos. Ymir's skull became the sky, with his brains as clouds. Sparks from Muspelheim were hurled up to become the stars.

Ymir's flesh was made into the earth; mountains were formed from his bones, and grass and trees from his hair. The oceans were formed from Ymir's sweat – or possibly blood, as in some versions of the myth. Worms (or maggots) emerged from the corpse of Ymir, and became beings known as dwarfs. Four of these were instructed to hold up the sky and prevent it from falling. They were named Nordi, Sundri, Austri and Vestri, corresponding to their positions in the north, south, east and west of the world. Other dwarfs emerged and went to live in an underground realm called Nidavellir.

The sun and the moon came to be when the Aesir were angered by the arrogance of a human. He had named his children Sol and Mani, in honour of their brightness and beauty. The gods punished this by exiling the children to the sky where they would ride in chariots carrying the sun and moon. The Jotunn Nat and her son Dag (night and day) were also sent into the sky aboard chariots of their own to ride around the world. The sun and moon were pursued by two wolves. These were the children of Jotnar, named Skoll and Hati Hrodvitnisson, and were destined to chase the sun and moon until the day of Ragnarok, when they would finally catch and devour them.

THE WORLD OF NORSE MYTH BEGAN WITH AN ACT OF VIOLENT CREATION; THE SLAYING OF YMIR AND DISMEMBERMENT OF HIS CORPSE.

## Yggdrasil, the World Tree

The actions of Odin and his brothers resulted in the creation of Nine Worlds, all connected by Yggdrasil, the World Tree. Yggdrasil, a great ash tree, lay at the centre of all worlds, touching all of them, although it could not be seen or perceived by mortals. Its roots reached out to other worlds – Asgard, Jotunheim and Niflheim – and close to each root there was a well. These 'wells' are sometimes referred to as springs; either

OPPOSITE: Sol and Mani were human children punished for their father's arrogance by having to ride in chariots endlessly around the world. They were pursued by wolves destined to catch them in the last days of the world.

ABOVE: Many attempts have been made to represent the multiple worlds of Norse myth and Yggdrasil, the great tree that linked them. The Bifrost bridge from Asgard to Midgard is also depicted here.

way, they are a source of waters and not necessarily a well in the sense of an artificial construction.

Yggdrasil provided the structure of the universe and also connected the Nine Worlds, enabling some to move between them – Odin did so by riding his horse Sleipnir along the trunk. Yggdrasil was eternal, and survived even Ragnarok. The last two humans were sheltered by Yggdrasil from the destruction of the world and emerged afterwards to repopulate the new one.

By the root reaching into Asgard was Urd's Well, sometimes called the Well of Wyrd or the Well of Destiny. Urd's Well was a source of great power and knowledge, from which Odin gained the runes. It also nourished the tree Yggdrasil and was in turn replenished by dewdrops falling from the tree. By this well the gods would meet, and it was also used by the three Norns.

The Norns were three mystical women, in many ways similar to the Greek Fates. However, although like the Fates they were connected with the destiny of every living thing, their predictions were not immutable. The Norns inscribed the destiny of each creature upon the trunk of Yggdrasil, but mortals did have some ability to alter their fate – the carvings could be rewritten depending on the actions of the subject.

LEFT: The Norns were supernatural beings associated with fate or destiny, but did not fully preordain a person's life. Instead, they watched over the range of possibilities available to that person, who could to some extent control his own fate.

The ability to control one's fate was connected with the cycle of water from the Well of Urd, which reflected the past, to the tree Yggdrasil and then back to the well. However, the initial carving of the Norns defined the range of possibilities and even the most powerful being could not change his fate to have an outcome beyond that range. Thus, where in Greek mythology a being's whole destiny was rigidly defined by the Fates, in Norse mythology the Norns essentially dealt a hand of cards and let the subject decide how to play them.

The second root ran into Jotunheim, where the Ginnungagap had previously been. Nearby lay the Mimir's Well, which contained great wisdom and intellect. It was here that Odin received his knowledge, although Mimir, the guardian of the well, would not permit him to drink until he placed one of his eyes in the well as an offering.

Mimir was a god of the Aesir tribe, renowned for his great wisdom. This was gained by drinking from his well, using a horn named Gjallarhorn. A horn of the same name was used by Heimdall to signal the approach of the Jotnar and the beginning of Ragnarok, although it is unclear if this is the same Gjallarhorn. Mimir was beheaded by the Vanir during their conflict with the Aesir and his head was sent to Odin, who used magic to keep it alive. Afterwards, Mimir's head still revealed secrets and gave counsel to Odin.

BELOW: Depictions of Yggdrasil and the great wolf Fenrir, who was destined to slay Odin during the final battle of Ragnarok. The various creatures that lived in the branches of Yggdrasil are also shown.

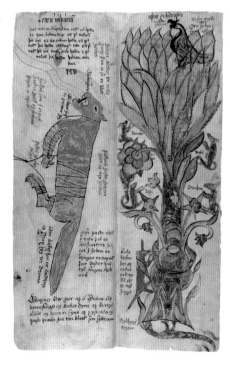

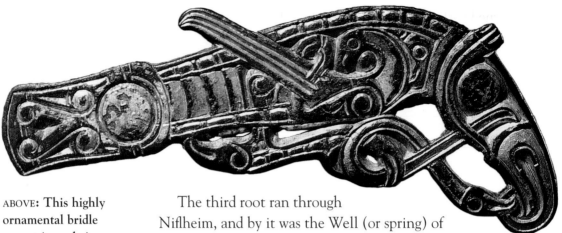

The third root ran through Niflheim, and by it was the Well (or spring) of Hvergelmir. This was the source of several rivers, and was replenished by liquid dripping from the horns of the stag Eikthyrinr. Eikthyrinr stood atop Odin's hall (the hall of Valhol where heroic warriors went after death) and fed from the foliage of Yggdrasil. Hvergelmir does not appear to have had magical properties as such, but it was so full of snakes that no language had a word for how many there were. Nearby lived the dragon Niohoggr (Nidhogg), who gnawed on the root of Yggdrasil and the corpses of the dead.

## CREATURES OF YGGDRASIL

In addition to the dragon Niohoggr, Yggdrasil was home to other creatures. Notable among them was an eagle who lived at the very top of Yggdrasil, whereas the dragon was – according to some interpretations – pinned down by the root. The eagle and the dragon were bitter enemies, not merely due to their very different situations. A squirrel named Ratatosk also lived in the tree, and made it his business to inform each of the two what the other had said. Thus insult and counter-insult were passed up and down the trunk of Yggdrasil, across the whole breadth of the Nine Worlds, ensuring that the eagle and dragon hated one another for all eternity. This was apparently for no better reason than Ratatosk's amusement. Four stags also lived in the branches of Yggdrasil, feeding upon the foliage.

## The Nine Worlds

It is commonly accepted that there were Nine Worlds in Norse mythos, but the reality is far more complex. There are direct references to the Nine Worlds and also inferences from other passages that suggest there were nine based upon the people that dwell in them. Seven races are described as having worlds or inhabiting a particular world; these plus the realms of Muspelheim and Niflheim make nine.

The goddess Hel is stated in the Eddas to have had authority over the Nine Worlds. Since she was concerned with the dead, and all things die, this seems to strongly imply that her authority covered everyone and everything that died in the whole cosmos. By this logic the Nine Worlds must therefore be the whole of the cosmos.

It seems fairly clear that there are nine main realms. However, within some of these there are areas with very different characteristics. The realm of the goddess Hel, for example, is sometimes stated to have lain within Niflheim and sometimes seems to be a separate place. Some sources seem confused on this matter, but even if Hel's realm lay in Niflheim, Niflheim itself was not Hel's realm. Her domain was surrounded by a high wall and was separate from the rest of Niflheim. Other worlds had regions ruled by gods or Jotnar, which were sometimes mistakenly thought to be whole worlds in their own right.

The existence of these sub-realms greatly confuses the issue, and even the relationship of one world to another is difficult to discern. The sources are at times contradictory, and as a result numerous attempts have been made to represent the relationship of the Nine Worlds, not all of which agree with one another. The situation is further complicated by the fact that some locations associated with the Aesir are actually in other realms.

BELOW: **In this depiction of the cosmos Midgard is protected by a wall and surrounded by ocean, within which lies the vast serpent Jormungand. Jormungand was so huge that he encircled the world and could eat his own tail.**

Some versions have the Nine Worlds arranged in three neat layers of three worlds, with the 'godly' realms at the top above the 'mortal' realms in the middle and the 'underworlds' in the bottom layer. Artists have struggled with the concept of the three great roots of Yggdrasil, since the roots of a normal tree are at the bottom, yet Yggdrasil has one reaching into Asgard, one into the mortal realms and one into the underworld. Artists have also come to various conclusions about whether to portray the underworld as above or below the main roots of the world tree, and whether the godly realms should be above, below or perched within the branches.

The main problem with this is that artists are attempting to create a literal representation of a metaphysical concept. Yggdrasil is present in all the worlds in a spiritual sense rather than as a physical tree of cosmic proportions growing up through the middle of the world. It is sometimes said to be at the 'centre' of a world, but 'heart' – in the spiritual sense – might be a better interpretation. It touches everything, creating a framework of

reality and a means of moving from one world to another, as well as a medium by which the waters of the Well of Urd interact with all things and influence their destiny. It may be simpler to think of Yggdrasil as an 'invisible cosmic framework' connecting the worlds than to try to represent it as something that actually looks like a tree.

One key concept throughout the Nine Worlds was that of 'innangard' and its opposite 'utangard'. Innangard can be translated as 'within the fence' or 'within the enclosure'. The nature of this enclosure is both physical and metaphysical – a place that was innangard obeyed reliable laws of nature and of men; somewhere that was utangard was less tame.

On a very mundane level, the area around a Norseman's stead or a village was innangard. It might or might not have a physical fence, but it had laws that had to be obeyed. Close to such a place, it was generally safe to go about your business; armed men were available to enforce the law or to drive off wild beasts. Further afield, beyond the physical and spiritual 'enclosure', the

LEFT: This tombstone depicts the first four dwarfs, who were assigned by the gods to stand at the corners of the world and hold up the sky. This may be a creation scene or a representation of the later cosmos.

land was wilder and contained many dangers. Outlaws, dwelling away from the settlements where the law was enforced, wild animals and mundane threats such as cold from which there might be no shelter posed a real danger to anyone venturing away from the innangard places.

## THE GODS SOUGHT POWER AND WISDOM IN WILD PLACES, BUT RETURNED TO THEIR SAFE ENCLOSURE IN ASGARD TO REST.

The concept of innangard and utangard ran right through the Norse mindset. Crops sown where a farmer wanted them were innangard, as were herds that grazed where he put them. A wild forest where dangers might lurk was utangard. Yet utangard was not necessarily bad. In the wilderness beyond civilization, power could be obtained. Thus the gods in many of their tales seek wisdom in wild and dangerous places and, of course, the ultimate source of all life, the Ginnungagap, was as utangard as it was possible to be.

Attitudes to laws and behaviour were influenced by these concepts. For example, the taking of slaves was forbidden, as was harming women and children – but only within the Norse lands themselves. Plunder, destruction and the taking of slaves were commonplace when on a raiding expedition. Thus the homelands were innangard, where the law applied, but different conduct was acceptable when in a place that was utangard.

This parallels the behaviour of the gods; a man who ventured beyond the safe enclosure of law and tamed land into utangard places could win riches through trade or raiding, although he also faced dangers along the way. At times it was necessary for men and gods to venture out into utangard places to defeat a threat and protect the innangard. Indeed, the safe, lawful places had to be defended constantly, since utangard was more of a natural state and chaos would creep into the innangard world if it was not pushed back.

It is notable that most of the Nine Worlds have names that end in 'heim', i.e. 'home'. Only Asgard and Midgard differ. Asgard is the most innangard a place can be – bounded by defensive walls and ruled by the Aesir gods. Midgard, the home of humans, was protected by a fence created by Odin and his brothers, and was in many ways a reflection of Asgard. Midgard was a (relatively) safe place for humans to exist, obeying predicable natural laws and fenced off from the wilderness outside. The other realms could be places of wildness and terror for humans; in many cases, a mortal could not even survive there without divine assistance.

The realm of the giants is known as Jotunheim, and also at times as Utgard. It is the personification of the concept of utangard – wild, unpredictable and full of danger, but also a place where power and wisdom can be obtained by those strong enough to take them. The Jotnar themselves are also utangard – they are wild, chaotic and do not obey the laws of the gods.

As a result of conflicting sources, there are more than nine candidates for inclusion among the Nine Worlds. Some apparently separate worlds may in fact be other names for the same place. The primary candidates are listed below.

## Realm of Asgard

Asgard was the home of the Aesir tribe of gods. It is generally depicted as lying above the mortal realms, connected to the human world of Midgard by Bifrost, the rainbow bridge. Asgard was a land of forests and rivers inhabited by both mundane and mystical creatures, surrounding the great city of the Aesir. Within this lay the palaces of Odin and his wife Frigga, as well as the abodes of other gods. The city of the Aesir is described as a place of gold and silver spires.

Also within Asgard lay the hall of Valhol, where heroic warriors waited for the day they would be called to battle at Ragnarok. Valhol was a wondrous place, with an everlasting supply of mead provided by a goat called Heidrun that stood on the roof. This allowed Heidrun to reach the leaves of the world tree Yggdrasil, upon which it fed while mead ran from its udders to be collected in a tub placed beneath. Also within the hall of Valhol was Saehriminir, a giant pig of magical properties from whom endless meat could be cut.

In some interpretations of the Eddas, Asgard is actually on Earth and is explicitly located as the city of Troy at one point. However, the Well of Urd where the gods hold their meetings is in the heavens, reached by crossing the Bifrost bridge.

## Realm of Vanaheim

Vanaheim was the home of the Vanir, a tribe of gods more associated with fertility and nature than the Aesir. According to some sources, Vanaheim lay to the west of Asgard; it is usually represented as one of the 'celestial' realms in the upper branches of Yggdrasil or above them. Relatively little is known about Vanaheim from the surviving sources, but some details can be inferred.

Like Asgard, Vanaheim was a realm of light and beauty, with forests and rivers filled with natural and supernatural creatures. It seems that Vanaheim may have been 'wilder' than Asgard, in the sense of being less urbanized and closer to nature. It might even have been quite a dangerous place for those not in harmony with the natural world, but the Vanir themselves belonged in such an environment and would have been quite at home. Vanaheim seems not to have been walled or fortified in the way that Asgard was.

## Realm of Alfheim

The third of the 'celestial' realms usually depicted as above the mortal world was Alfheim, home to the Light Elves. These were powerful beings, perhaps minor gods, with powers over nature and fertility. Alfheim lay close to Asgard and was relatively easy to get to from there. Similarly to Vanaheim, it was a wild land of forests and animals, probably dangerous for those who did not belong there.

Alfheim was ruled by the god Freyr, who was one of the Vanir. This suggests a close relationship between the Light Elves and the Vanir, although its exact nature is not made clear in the original sources.

## Realm of Midgard

Midgard was the world of mortals, and the only realm that could be completely perceived by humans. It was surrounded by seas, which are stated in the Eddas to be impossible to cross. In these oceans lay the great serpent Jormangandr, who was so huge that his body encircled the world. Midgard was also bounded by a great wall made from the eyebrows or eyelashes of the giant Ymir. This kept out the Jotnar and ensured that Midgard, like Asgard, remained innangard.

Midgard was connected to Asgard by Yggdrasil and also directly by means of Bifrost, the rainbow bridge. Although Midgard obeyed the laws of the gods, it had its dangers. However, these were of a mundane sort, which humans at least stand a chance against. That situation would change at Ragnarok, when the gods came to the plain of Vigrid to fight the Jotnar. At that time, Midgard would be destroyed and almost everything in it would perish.

## Realm of Jotunheim

Jotunheim lay in the 'middle world' alongside Midgard, but is also noted as lying on the south bank of the river Iving, which separated it from Asgard. It was a barren and cold land, and can be taken as a prime example of the concept of utangard, which can mean 'beyond the law' or 'outside the fence', i.e. beyond the world that is safe and sane by the standards of ordinary men. Jotunheim is sometimes called Utgard, although this also refers to its capital, a city carved from ice.

Although the Jotnar were in general hostile to the gods, there are sometimes peaceful or at least non-violent interactions between them; many of the gods married giantesses, and at times the gods journeyed into Jotunheim to seek treasures or wisdom. A root of Yggdrasil reached into Jotunheim, and close to it lay Mimir's Well. At one time, Mimir was the guardian of this well and could be found close by, suggesting that it was possible for a god to live in the land of the Jotnar.

ABOVE: Freyr was a member of the Vanir tribe, but joined the Aesir at the end of the war between the gods. He was a popular god associated with fertility and good harvests, and was described as being 'hated by none'.

## Realm of Muspelheim

Muspelheim lay in the south of the world. It was a land of fire, ruled by the fire giant Surt and his kin, the Eldjotnar. It is also home to fire demons. It can be inferred from the creation tale that rivers of lava flowed through and perhaps out of Muspelheim, and showers of sparks were not uncommon. Few other details of the place are presented, however.

## Realm of Niflheim

In the north of the world lay Niflheim, a frozen land that was the first of the Nine Worlds to be created. It contained the oldest of the three great wells: Hvergelmir. From this source came all the cold waters of the world. A root of Yggdrasil extended into Niflheim, where it was gnawed by the dragon Nidhogg. Nidhogg also tormented the dead, eating their corpses or sucking the blood from them. Niflheim was the origin of the Hrimthursar (frost giants) and beings named Niflungar. These are referred to as Nibelungs in Wagner's 'Ring Cycle'.

## Realm of Nidavellir

Nidavellir was the underground home of the Dwarfs, who made great magical devices and weapons. It consisted of a maze of mines and underground workshops. It is possible that Nidavellir and Svartalfheim are in fact the same place – the distinction between Dwarfs and Dark Elves is somewhat vague at times.

RIGHT: This colourful depiction shows the Bifrost bridge linking Asgard to Midgard.

## Realm of Svartalfheim

Another underground realm, Svartalfheim was the home of
the Dark Elves, mischievous creatures widely believed to be
responsible for nightmares. The Dark Elves were turned to stone
by the sun's rays, so they made their home in the underworld.

## Realm of Hel, or Helheim

Some sources suggest that the goddess Hel had her realm in
Niflheim, but that she did not rule all of it. Her domain, known
as Niflhel, was walled off from the rest of Niflheim. It was a land
of cold fog, but was less icy than other parts of the realm. Other
versions of the myths consider Helheim to be a separate realm,
usually depicted as being deep underground. However, this may
be due to Christian influences on later scholars – Hel simply
means 'concealed' or 'hidden', and there are no clear indications
that Hel was in fact located deep in the Earth.

## The Bifrost Bridge

The Bifrost bridge linked Asgard to Midgard. It appeared as
a rainbow, and its name has connotations of a 'trembling' or
'fleeting' bridge, suggesting that it is not permanently fixed. In
some versions of Norse mythology, the gods mostly lived on
Earth and travelled over Bifrost each day to reach Asgard, before
returning home at night.

Although allowing quick and easy access to the mortal realms,
Bifrost was a potential weak point in the defences of Asgard,
and must be watched constantly. This was the task of the god
Heimdall, whose mission was to warn the gods if the Jotnar
approached the bridge. On the day of Ragnarok he would blow
his horn to summon the gods to battle, but this could not prevent
the Jotnar from storming Asgard. Their passage over Bifrost
caused its destruction.

## Ragnarok and the Renewing of the World

Norse mythology is cyclical, and contains many examples of
cyclic events such as the waters from Urd's Well nourishing the
tree Yggdrasil then returning to the well. The world itself cannot
be eternal; it must eventually be destroyed and made anew.

The story of Ragnarok and the destruction of the world seems, at first glance, to be rather gloomy. The battle destroys the world, the gods die and, worst of all, they have foreknowledge of it, but cannot alter their fate. Yet there is more to it than that. For one thing, the 'Twilight of the Gods' as the end of the world is sometimes called, provides a fitting end to the stories of the gods. Just as Norse warriors hoped to meet a glorious end in battle and earn a place in Valhol, the tale of the great warrior god Thor should not end in old age and sickness.

Instead, the gods meet a glorious end defending their world against the forces of utangard, who have come to return it to a state of chaos uninhabitable by mortals. Thor dies, but only after defeating the giant serpent Jormangandr. He lives long enough to know he has won his greatest victory and that those sheltering behind him are safe. To the Norse mindset, there can be no better way to go. Likewise, dutiful and steadfast Heimdall and treacherous Loki slay one another. Odin is killed by the wolf Fenrir, but the Allfather is immediately avenged by his son.

The tales of the Norse gods are big stories, and the battle of Ragnarok provides a fitting end to them. The gods (all but Loki, but he was a Jotunn first and last) are true to their nature to the very end, fighting and dying to protect the world they made. And because of this steadfastness, Ragnarok is not the end.

The Fire Jotnar burn Asgard and break the world, and monsters run amok causing more chaos and destruction. The world is ruined and sinks into the sea, and even Yggdrasil is set on fire. But afterward, there are survivors. Some of the gods and the mortal heroes from Valhol come through the fighting alive, and thus earn themselves a place in the new creation. The last two mortal humans are sheltered by Yggdrasil, and when the world rises out of the sea made anew, they take their place in it.

OPPOSITE: Thor was destined to slay and be slain by the great serpent Jormungand, but chose to seek it out rather than waiting for the fateful encounter. His attempt to fish for Jormungand in the boat of Hymir the Jotunn was ultimately unsuccessful.

## THE CREATION OF THE NEW WORLD

Most people think of Ragnarok as the battle at the end of everything, but in fact it is the catastrophic act of destruction needed to renew the world. As the slaying of Ymir permitted the creation of the world in the first place, Ragnarok allows its ills to be swept away and replaced with something fresh, new and wonderful.

Far from being the gloomy, nihilistic 'end of all things', Ragnarok can be viewed as the triumph of hope and courage, a final test rather than an ending. Those that survive earn a place in a better world than the present one. True, the cost is very high, but the Norse mythos is all about striving, braving great dangers and suffering great loss in return for a chance to make things better.

2

# THE DEITIES

Norse mythology is unusual in that it has two sets of deities who became a single pantheon. This is thought by some scholars to represent a clash between two rival religions, perhaps due to different groups coming together to create proto-Norse society, or the triumph of new arrivals (and their gods) over the existing religion of Scandinavia.

The clash between the Aesir (gods of war) and Vanir (gods of nature or fertility) could have a different mythic significance, however. It might indicate a change in society to a more martial outlook, since although the two sets of gods are supposedly equal the Aesir seem to be the senior partners.

There are other indications that displacement of an earlier religion took place. The Light Elves (Ljosalfar) are sometimes presented as minor deities or powerful spirits, and there are intimations that they were once more powerful, but were displaced (apparently without much conflict) by the current set of gods. The Jotnar, on the other hand, were enemies of the gods right from the start. One of Odin's earliest acts was to slay Ymir and prevent more Jotnar from being created, because he feared

OPPOSITE: Odin is depicted here with his magical spear Gungnir. The winged helm is an affectation of much later artists, who sought to romanticize the Norsemen as they had the Greeks and Romans.

BELOW: **A one-eyed bronze figurine of Odin, from the Statens Historika Museum, Stockholm.**

that they would dominate the cosmos. Two Frost Jotnar survived to recreate their race, and the Fire Jotnar were not affected by the death of Ymir.

Thus the Norse mythos contained two sets of gods who joined together, another set of former gods who were apparently content to be powerful supernatural creatures who did not exert much influence over the cosmos, and two sets of gods-in-all-but-name who were the sworn enemies of the current deities. There were also numerous monsters and other beings that are of supernatural or divine origins, many of which are the offspring of gods, Jotunn or both.

## The Aesir

The Aesir were the foremost of the two tribes of gods. They were concerned mainly with war and martial virtues, which translates to the ruler-protector role of the upper echelons of Norse society. The origin of the word 'Aesir' is not totally clear, but it probably comes from the proto-Germanic language with connotations of natural forces or the natural order of things. Male Aesir are known as Ass (plural Aesir) and females are known as Asynja (plural Asynjur). The Aesir dwelt in Asgard, which is said to be located at the top of the world tree Yggdrasil.

It can be argued that the Aesir take the role of the husband in what can be viewed as a 'marriage' between the Aesir and the Vanir. In traditional Norse society, women were forbidden to cut their hair short or wear men's clothing, and particularly to use weapons. On the other hand, it was forbidden to do harm to a woman. The husband was responsible for making business deals, speaking at gatherings and fighting when necessary, roles that were reflected to some extent at least in the characteristics of the Aesir gods.

## Odin

Odin the Allfather was the chief of the Aesir, and thus of all the gods. He was a very complex character, who displayed a number of traits more associated with the concept of utangard than might be expected from the maker of the world and the giver of laws. Despite being the leader of the gods, he had a tendency to wander off on personal quests, usually in search of wisdom or to further his own goals.

Known as Woden or Wotan in other Germanic and Anglo-Saxon tongues, Odin gave his name to the day Wednesday, and was husband to the goddess Frigg, one of the Asynjur. With Frigg he had the sons Baldr and Hod; his other sons include Thor, Heimdall and Tyr. Odin is also the spiritual father of all humanity – it was he that began the work of creating the first humans after slaying the giant Ymir.

Odin was a powerful warrior, but could also perform magic, which is generally considered in Norse mythology to be effeminate. Similarly, his demeanour could change rapidly – he was a good and friendly companion when he wanted to be, and a terrifying threat if roused to anger or displeasure. He is often portrayed rather one-dimensionally as a wise and noble king, but in fact he was devious and capable of treachery when it suited his purposes. One of his first acts was to murder the Jotunn Ymir while he slept. Odin's self-sacrifice, hanging impaled on a tree while seeking wisdom, was not a selfless act. He chose to suffer in order to obtain power for himself, later sacrificing one of his own eyes in order to obtain precious knowledge.

Odin was associated with inspiration and fury; his was a lunacy of greatness rather than the dignity of a king. He was thus a god to be feared and respected rather than loved, and he was not very concerned with the vast masses of ordinary people. Odin respected those who stood above others; he was the patron of many great warriors and, oddly perhaps, also of outcasts and outlaws. Although he was the leader of the gods, he was willing to help those who disregarded the law and lived outside it. This is in keeping with his own wild nature – Odin was willing to plunge into chaos if it furthered his goals, and understood the necessity of the utangard as part of the world.

BELOW: Odin's self-sacrifice was not for the betterment of others; he spent nine days impaled on a spear and hanging from the tree Yggdrasil to further his own ends. Such a harsh god had little time for ordinary people.

Odin is also associated with poetry – indeed, he spoke in poems. He controlled the Mead of Poetry, which he stole by means of trickery from the giant Suttung. He allowed others to partake of the mead if he felt them worthy, enabling them to become poets or scholars and to use great powers of persuasion. Several of the saga-heroes are warrior-poets claiming Odin as their patron or their inspiration.

Odin's verses included a great deal of wisdom on various subjects, much of which was concerned with advice for living a successful life or avoiding having it cut short by enemies. Thus Odin advised on subjects ranging from winning friends and seducing women to checking for ambushes before entering a building. Among his most important pronouncements was a verse connected with the Norse concept of 'Wordfame'. Essentially, Odin pointed out that all things perish and possessions become meaningless, but a man's 'Wordfame' – the judgement of his actions by others – lives on long after his death. Norse people were very concerned with the opinion of others, both during and after their lifetime, and held that a short but remarkable life was superior to long decades of mediocrity.

BELOW: **Mimir was extremely wise and may have been the mysterious uncle who taught Odin his songs of power. After he was decapitated, his head lived on and was able to offer Odin counsel on many matters.**

In addition to the Mead of Poetry, Odin had other magical treasures. One of them was the head of Mimir, a wise god who was decapitated during the conflict between the Aesir and the Vanir. Mimir's head was enchanted by Odin to prevent rot, and revealed secrets when asked for counsel. Odin also had a magical spear named Gungnir, made by Dwarfs from the wood of Yggdrasil and further enchanted by Odin with magical runes.

As befits such a great personage, Odin was accompanied by magical creatures. The ravens Hugin (Thought) and Munin (Desire, but sometimes translated as 'Memory' instead) were beings in their own right, but also a personification of Odin's thoughts and desires. His eight-legged horse, Sleipnir, was described as the best of horses and became the father of many heroes' mounts. The Valkyries, too, are independent beings, but also the personification of some aspects of Odin. Like Odin they were capable of both helping and harming mortals – they guided the heroic dead to Valhol, but also sometimes cast curses to impede warriors in battle.

Odin's patronage of heroes was, like most of his other actions, less than selfless. The best of the dead were taken to Valhol, Odin's home, where they waited for the day of Ragnarok. This can be seen as a reward for heroism, but it was also self-interest on Odin's part – he was holding ready an army of heroes to assist him in his greatest battle. Odin is also associated with the 'Wild Hunt', in which the dead or supernatural beings (or both) pursued a quarry across the sky. Its appearance was generally thought to presage disaster.

ABOVE: **Odin's ravens were separate beings, but also aspects of his own. He did worry about them when they flew out each day to gather news for him, fearing that they might come to some harm.**

Odin had two brothers, Vili and Ve, who feature in two tales about his life. They could be aspects of Odin himself rather than actual brothers, but it does seem that they could be in places where Odin was not. Vili and Ve fought and killed the giant Ymir alongside Odin, and helped him make the world out of Ymir's corpse before disappearing into obscurity. There is only one other mention of them, in a tale where Odin is exiled from Asgard by the other gods. He had made such a nuisance of himself in Midgard that the gods feared the bad opinion of humans, and exiled Odin for ten years. During this time Vili and Ve slept with Odin's wife Frigg.

## ODIN'S BROTHERS VILI AND VE MAY HAVE BEEN SEPARATE ENTITIES, ASPECTS OF ODIN'S PERSONALITY.

This tale could be literal – the Norse gods were not known for their monogamous relationships or excessive faithfulness – but could also be a metaphor for Odin changing his ways for a time. Odin, Vili and Ve are identified with three aspects of the god's character: Odin is ecstasy (inspiration or fury), Vili is conscious intention or will and Ve is holy or sacred. Thus this tale might imply that Odin's inspired fury was absent from Asgard, making things rather calmer in his household.

The idea that Odin (or at least his inspired fury) might be exiled from Asgard reflects the Norse concern with Wordfame and the relationship between gods and humans. Men and women would threaten or curse the gods if things did not go their way, and even the gods cared about what was said of them.

Odin thus fulfilled several roles in the Norse pantheon. He was the chief of the gods but also a patron of outlaws; the Allfather but also a practitioner of womanly magic. He was associated with war but not as the 'honourable warrior' so much as an inspired or furious slayer, and was more concerned with death than fighting. A brilliant intellect and a great poet, he was selfish and passionate rather than logical. If Odin can be summed up simply at all, it is by saying that he was the personification of self-will and the belief that greatness placed him above the law.

BELOW: **Odin's horse Sleipnir was the father of many great horses associated with mortal heroes. He was able to travel between worlds by galloping along the trunk and branches of Yggdrasil.**

# Frigg

Frigg was the wife of Odin and a powerful practitioner of Seidr magic. This was mainly concerned with determining fate and destiny, although Frigg does not seem to have imparted much of her knowledge to others. There is little information on her activities in the traditional sources, but it is possible that she served the gods as an advisor. This would parallel accounts from the pre-Viking Age in which the wife of a war-leader foretold the outcome of conflict through omens and could sometimes influence events with her magic.

One of Frigg's deeds was truly epic in scale, although it took place in the background of another story and is often glossed over. Fearing for the safety of her son Baldr, she secured an oath from every living thing in the cosmos not to hurt him. In the event, she overlooked one – mistletoe – that proved to be Baldr's downfall, but nevertheless this was an enormous undertaking.

Frigg's home was Fensalir, which translates as 'Fen halls'. She was associated with wetlands and marshes, which may have connections to early religious practices, such as placing sacrifices in marsh. In her home at Fensalir, Frigg met a mysterious woman who said she had noted how nothing seemed to harm Baldr, and Frigg

BELOW: Frigg was a powerful goddess whose arguments with her husband Odin at times resulted in adventures and misfortune for mortals. She was sufficiently influential to be able to obtain an oath from all living things not to harm her son Baldr.

told the woman of the oath extracted from all things, and even of the exception. This was a mistake, for the woman was Loki in disguise and he used this knowledge to engineer Baldr's murder.

Frigg is often confused with Freya, since both goddesses have virtually identical powers and names. This is not coincidental; both originated from the same goddess in the proto-Norse religion, whose name was Frija. Similarly, it has been variously asserted that Frigg or Freya is the origin of the day Friday, but it is more likely that Frija – the original form of both – was the source of the name.

## Tyr

Tyr was a war-god who may have been far more important in pre-Norse religion. He was eclipsed by Odin by the 'Viking Age', but was probably the original leader of the gods. This does not mean that there are tales of how Odin usurped Tyr's powers by trickery and magic – although they would surely be good ones! Instead, it simply means that at some time before the Viking Age Tyr was worshipped as the greatest of the Norse gods, but later Odin was revered in that position. Since the tales that are told about the gods are in effect the 'reality' of the situation, in the 'Viking Age' Odin was and had always been the creator of the world and leader of the gods, but there was a time when there might have been a tale of how Tyr performed similar deeds.

ABOVE: The war god Tyr was an honourable and straightforward being, well suited to leading a warband, but lacking the deviousness required of a king. There is evidence that he was supplanted by Odin as leader of the gods.

Tyr gave his name to Tuesday, and was associated by Roman observers with Mars. However, this was an outsider's viewpoint only – Tyr was Tyr, not Mars, although they had much in common. Tyr was good at starting fights, but could only end them through violence; he was no peacemaker. He was extremely brave and despite his reputation for honourable conduct could take part in a necessary deception. It seems that he placed the common good above the requirement for complete honesty, but only in dire circumstances.

When the gods wanted to bind the great wolf Fenrir they could not do so by force, but instead had to persuade Fenrir to agree to be bound. This was done in the form of a bet – not an uncommon event in Norse mythology – the gist of which was that Fenrir believed nothing could bind him; the gods bet him that they had found something that could. Fenrir would only agree if the gods promised to untie him if they were successful. To guarantee this promise, one of the gods must place his hand in Fenrir's mouth, essentially offering the great wolf the chance to bite it off if he was betrayed.

Tyr, of course, knew what was about to happen – Fenrir was indeed going to be betrayed and his hand would be lost. Yet he placed his hand in the wolf's mouth as security, and Fenrir was reassured. When the gods refused to unbind Fenrir, Tyr lost his hand as the price of ridding the cosmos of a destructive monster – at least for a time.

This participation in the deception of Fenrir seems slightly at odds with Tyr's reputation as an honourable warrior and lawgiver. However, this is explained by the Norse attitude to innangard and utangard, and how it related to their own people and outsiders. Conduct that was forbidden against Norse people (such as taking slaves or harming women) was acceptable in a raid or war against outsiders. It may be that the same concept applied to laws and oaths – they were only relevant to the Norse people themselves, and less binding regarding promises made to outsiders.

BELOW: Many cultures considered that a man who was disfigured or who had a missing body part was unfit to rule. The loss of Tyr's hand would thus make him ineligible for leadership of the gods.

Some might justify the participation of Tyr in the deception of Fenrir as a fair bargain – the deal was that the wolf would bite off a god's hand if he remained bound, and Tyr paid the price as agreed. If the bargain was not to Fenrir's liking he should not have made it in the first place. It may also be that Tyr was a guardian of his people and willing to do what was necessary to protect them, even if that meant treachery against the utangard outsider Fenrir. In other words, his duty was to protect his people from the wolf and this was the means by which it could be done. For a god as honourable and courageous as Tyr, there was no choice to be made – he was loyal first and foremost to his own.

It has been suggested that this tale accounts for Tyr's eclipse by Odin. Tyr was a straightforward, honest god, representing someone who made a good leader when populations were small. A person in Tyr's image could run a farmstead or lead a small settlement effectively, but as society evolved it became necessary to take decisions that were more grey than black and white. The cunning, sometimes deceitful rulership of a king was needed more than the honest word of a simple leader. The replacement of Tyr by Odin as leader of the gods may have been a metaphor for the changing nature of Norse society, with the loss of Tyr's hand as a symbol of his waning power.

# THOR – BRAWN VS BRAINS

Thor was a mighty warrior, but not a great thinker. The tales of his adventures include several incidents in which he was outwitted, including one where he not only failed to recognize a stranger as his father Odin, despite spending considerable time trading threats, boasts and insults. Thor generally met his problems head-on and smashed them with his hammer; fighting was his main talent, although he also commanded storms and lightning.

## Thor

Thor was the son of Odin. His mother may have been Jord, a Jotunn associated with the Earth, although some sources give her identity as either Fjorgyn or Hlodgyn. In any case, Thor's mother was a Jotunn and his father, Odin, was half Aesir and half Jotunn. Despite being more giant than god, Thor was a steadfast and loyal protector of Asgard and Midgard, who took the role of the premier war god among the Aesir. He gave his name to the day Thursday. Thor possessed several treasures, of

LEFT: A depiction of Thor with Mjolnir, though without his magical gauntlets and belt. Recent reinventions of the Thor character suggest that only someone worthy of ruling Asgard could wield Mjolnir, but the original version was simply very, very heavy.

which the most famous was the hammer Mjolnir. Despite his impressive physical strength, even Thor could not wield Mjolnir without the aid of his magical belt, which increased his strength, and his gauntlets. Although a mighty weapon, Mjolnir was also something of a badge of office, and was used by Thor to bless weddings, births and other events. The hammer was a near-universal symbol of the Norse religion, and continued to be worn as a good luck charm long after Christianity became prevalent.

Thor also possessed a magical chariot pulled by goats, although he did not always use it to get around. Some sources state that the gods lived on Earth and travelled on horseback over the Bifrost bridge every day to Asgard, except Thor who walked and took a different route. This required wading through boiling rivers for reasons that remain unclear. The goats could also be killed and eaten, then brought back to life when the chariot was needed. Thor dwelt with his wife Sif and their children in Asgard. His hall was named Bilskirnir, which means 'lightning crack'. It is sometimes referred to as the greatest building in all creation, which may reflect the fact that later in the 'Viking Age' Thor began to eclipse even Odin in importance. The settlers of Iceland venerated Thor above all others.

Thor had a daughter named Thrud with his wife Sif. A Valkyrie of the same name also existed, but it is not clear whether this was Thor's daughter or simply someone with the same name. Thor had two sons, Magni and Modi, by the giantess Jarnsaxa. After his death at Ragnaroks they inherited his hammer and survived into the new world created afterwards.

Although primarily a war god, Thor was also partially responsible for the fertility of the land. Farmers were as likely to appeal to him for a good rainstorm as warriors for aid in battle. Thor was far more egalitarian than his elitist father, Odin; a god of the people rather than being above them. Thus, while Odin chose the best of warriors and was little concerned with everybody else, Thor was often seen as a friend to the common fighting-man or farmer.

## Sif

Sif was Thor's wife, although relatively little was recorded about her. She was probably a personification of the earth, since pairings of sky and earth gods are common in Germanic and similar mythologies, and Sif's golden hair may be an allusion to fields of grain. This golden hair was cut off by the trickster Loki, which almost cost him his life. However, the outcome of this unpleasant incident seems to have satisfied everyone – Sif received new hair made by Dwarfs and the gods received other treasures, including Thor's hammer Mjolnir.

## Baldr

Baldr was the son of Odin and Frigg, and was loved by everything in creation. Baldr was so handsome and majestic that he glowed,

OPPOSITE: Baldr and his wife Nanna. Baldr was loved by everything in creation except, apparently, Loki. Even mistletoe did not mean him any harm. It had simply not been asked to make the oath not to harm Baldr.

and he was very precious to his mother. Thus when he began
to dream of his death, Frigg set about getting everything in the
cosmos to promise not to hurt him.

Baldr is often portrayed as a rather
innocent, passive god who was content
to be agreeable and nice, but this may
be a result of later Christian influences.
In the original tales there are several
references to his warlike nature. Being
(apparently) invulnerable to harm gave

## JUST AS TYR WAS ECLIPSED BY ODIN, THOR GRADUALLY BECAME MORE IMPORTANT THAN HIS FATHER.

him something of an unfair advantage in a fight, and he was
not hesitant to take this advantage. He also became involved
in a (perhaps foolish) game whereby the other gods would hurl
weapons and whatever else they could find at him. This bravado
was Baldr's undoing.

There was one exception to the oath not to harm Baldr.
Mistletoe, a small and apparently harmless thing, had not given
the oath and was therefore capable of hurting Baldr. Normally

this would not be much
of a problem; there was
a limit to how much
harm a piece of mistletoe
could do. However,
Loki – in his nastiest
trick of all – somehow
contrived to make a
spear from mistletoe and
gave it to Hod, Baldr's
blind brother. Hod cast
the spear and killed his
brother.

There is another
version of the same
story, in which Hod and
Baldr were warleaders who
clashed over the affections
of the goddess Nanna. Hod
obtained the power to defeat

ABOVE: Some versions of the tale have Baldr killed by an arrow rather than a javelin or spear. The gist is the same however; Loki tricks Hod into using a weapon made of mistletoe and even aims it for him.

OPPOSITE: Depictions of ancient gods change along with the societies that make them. This image of Heimdall reflects the times in which it was created far more than the original essence of the Bifrost guardian.

Baldr's invulnerability by journeying to the underworld, and was able to mortally wound him. In both tales, Hod was immediately struck down in vengeance for what he had done.

Baldr's death is significant in many ways. The traditional 'Viking funeral' in which a ship is either buried or cast adrift after being set on fire reflects the ceremony presided over by Odin to honour his fallen son. Grave-goods were placed in Baldr's pyre, again reflecting the practice of sending goods with the dead.

Loki's part in the murder of Baldr was only half of his cruellest trick. The other part was the way he forced Baldr to remain dead. So beloved was Baldr that when the gods asked Hel, goddess of the dead, to release him from her realm she agreed under the condition that every being in creation had to weep for Baldr. Everyone did, except a giantess named Thokk. Since the condition had not been fulfilled, Hel refused to release Baldr.

In fact, Thokk was Loki in disguise playing the second half of his trick. The gods were so angered that they savagely punished Loki, chaining him in a cave where a serpent's venom would fall upon him and burn him. This torment changed Loki from a troublesome trickster to the hate-filled enemy of the gods, and ultimately resulted in him leading the Jotnar against Asgard on the day of Ragnarok. Baldr came back to life after Ragnarok, bringing his beauty and majesty into the new world that was created afterwards.

## Heimdall

Heimdall was a son of Odin. He had nine mothers, although exactly how this came to be remains unclear. He seems at one time to have been credited with creating humanity and laying out the hierarchical structure (essentially leaders, warriors and farmers) of Norse society, although Odin is given the credit for this in most of the Norse myths that survive to this day.

Heimdall was a brave and loyal warrior, whose task was to watch and wait for the approach of the Jotnar. His senses were

so keen that he could see a hundred miles and hear the grass growing at the far end of the Bifrost bridge in Midgard. It is possible that he gained this ability by a sacrifice similar to Odin's loss of an eye in the Well of Mimir; there are references to something belonging to Heimdall being buried or hidden beneath Yggdrasil. This may be an ear or something less physical. Either way, Heimdall had supernaturally keen senses.

Heimdall was the enemy of Loki, whose wily nature was the polar opposite of the steadfast guardian. At Ragnarok, when the Jotunn led by Loki approached Asgard, Heimdall gave warning by blowing Gjallarhorn – a war horn that may also have been used for drinking – to call the gods out to battle. He then fought Loki to mutual destruction.

## Idun and Bragi

Idun was one of the most important goddesses of the Aesir as she tended the fruit that kept the gods youthful. Unlike many mythologies, Norse religion did not have immortal gods. They had very long lifespans, but without Idun's 'apples' they would grow old and die. Although many sources use the word 'apple'

BELOW: The gods were not immortal, but were kept young by magical fruits provided by the goddess Idun. The idea that these were apples is a later distortion; traditional references suggest a range of fruits.

LEFT: Loki is tricked and captured by the Jotunn Thjazi in the form of an eagle. Thjazi wanted the goddess Idun and her magical fruits, and forced Loki to help him capture her.

for Idun's fruits, this was probably not the original meaning. More than likely there were a variety of magical fruits that Idun looked after and dispensed to the gods; the term 'apple' is a later distortion.

Be that as it may, Idun's fruits were vital to the wellbeing of the gods and their ultimate survival. They were deprived of their magic once, when Idun was captured by the Jotunn Thjazi. This came about due to a trick played by Thjazi, although it would not have been possible without the hot-headed actions and fickleness of Loki.

While travelling with other gods, Loki encountered an eagle that prevented his dinner (a wild ox found in a desolate land)

from cooking by using magic. The eagle agreed to stop interfering with the gods' cookery in return for a share of the food, but then grabbed all the best bits of the ox for itself. Despite the fact that this sort of one-sided deal was Loki's stock in trade, he was angered to find that he had been tricked and grabbed a branch with which to attack the eagle.

The eagle seized the branch and flew off with it with Loki still attached. The eagle then revealed that he was in fact the Jotunn Thjazi in disguise, and would drop Loki to his death if he did not swear an oath to bring to Thjazi the goddess Idun and her magical fruit. Loki swore, and for whatever reason decided that keeping this promise was more important than preserving the immortality of himself and his fellow gods.

Loki returned to Asgard and persuaded the goddess to go with him to find some fruits that he claimed were even more wonderful than her own. She was borne off by the giant (again in the form of an eagle) and soon the gods began to feel the effects of old age. They correctly deduced that Loki was responsible and instructed him to make amends. If he failed, he would be killed.

THE KIDNAP OF IDUN WAS ONE OF THE MOST SERIOUS THREATS FACED BY THE GODS. WITHOUT HER THEY WOULD GROW OLD AND DIE.

Loki borrowed a magical set of hawk feathers from Freya and flew to Thjazi's stronghold in Jotunheim. There, he took advantage of the Jotunn's absence to turn Idun into a nut and carry her off. The giant gave chase, and might have caught Loki but for a huge fire built by the other gods. As Loki passed over the walls of Asgard, the gods lit their fire and incinerated the pursuing Jotunn. With Idun and her apples restored to them, the gods were made young again and Loki avoided execution.

Idun was married to Bragi, a poet and bard so great that he had runes on his tongue. There is an obscure reference to Idun sleeping with the murderer of her brother, but this accusation came from Loki and there are no details of the event, nor any other mention of a brother. Whether the murderer was supposed to be Bragi or some other god with whom Idun had a dalliance remains unclear.

Bragi was the patron of earthly bards and poets, and may have been a mortal bard who was given the status of a god in later tales. Bragi did not play a great part in the tales of the gods, but nevertheless fulfilled an important role in a society where tales of a god's or a person's deeds were a form of immortality and status.

## Other Aesir

Numerous other gods appear at times in the Norse tales, in many cases on a single occasion or only in passing as a companion of one of the other gods during an adventure or journey. Among these was Vali, avenger of Baldr. Vali was a son of Odin who was present when Hod was tricked into slaying Baldr. He immediately struck down Hod then disappeared from the tales until the day of

OPPOSITE: The god Ullr
was a great hunter who
was adept at using skis
and skates, but little else
is known about him.
He may have been a
proto-Norse god whose
worship had more or less
ceased by the 'Viking
Age'.

Ragnarok. His deeds at Ragnarok are not detailed, but he is listed among the survivors.

Another of Odin's sons was Vidar, who is referred to as the 'silent god' and does not appear in any stories until Odin is slain by the wolf Fenrir at Ragnarok. Vidar, who was apparently the strongest of all the gods except Thor, forced open Fenrir's jaws with his feet – he had magical shoes created for this specific purpose – and slew the wolf.

Among the other Aesir who appear from time to time in the tales is Forseti, who lived in a great palace of gold and silver and acted as a Lawspeaker for the gods. His role as judge and arbitrator echoes the role of Lawspeakers in traditional Icelandic society, but the only references to his deeds are fragmentary. The Icelandic politician and historian Snorri Sturluson records that Forseti was the son of Baldr and Nanna, but this is probably his

RIGHT: Vidar, son of
Odin, avenged his
father by pushing open
the jaws of Fenrir and
plunging his sword into
the great beast's heart.
He does not appear in
any other tales.

own invention as there is no traditional source for this assertion.

Snorri Sturluson also tells of the journey made by Hermod after Baldr was killed. Doubt has been shed on the origins of this tale, but it is possible that Sturluson had access to sources that have since been lost. Hermod was a warrior god, who undertook a journey to Helheim in the hope of rescuing Baldr. He made this journey with the assistance of Odin's eight-legged horse Sleipnir.

The god Hoenir appears in some tales travelling with Loki, but his nature is confusing. He is listed as one of the gods who gave gifts to Ask and Embla, the first humans, but the gift he gave was Odr. The story of the Mead of Poetry states that humans received Odr (ecstasy, frenzy or inspiration) from Odin himself, which confuses this issue somewhat. Hoenir does appear among the gods who survived Ragnarok.

Hoenir played an important role in the conflict between the Aesir and the Vanir as a hostage given to the Vanir. Here, he is portrayed as a handsome dimwit who relied too much on the counsel of Mimir. Despite being made chief among the Vanir, Hoenir was unable to make any useful decision without Mimir's advice, angering the Vanir to the point where they decapitated Mimir.

Along with Hoenir and Odin, Lodurr was the third god who gave gifts to Ask and Embla. Very little is known about Lodurr, other than that Odin was 'Lodurr's friend', but it is recorded that he gave Ask and Embla the gifts of good looks and something called La. This is often taken to mean 'warmth', but the word is not used elsewhere in this context. One possible interpretation is the warmth of life conferred by blood.

Another obscure god was Ullr, who seems to have been powerful at one time – Odin is promised Ullr's blessings in return for rescue from a difficult situation. However, little is recorded about Ullr's deeds. He was

the son of Sif and is noted as a great archer and hunter, who travelled by means of skis and skates. A kenning (a kind of word play that features in Norse poetry) used by bards refers to a shield as 'Ullr's ship', but the connotations of this are lost. It would seem that Ullr was an early Scandinavian god who is vaguely remembered as having been powerful, but whose tales have been lost.

## IT WAS COMMON FOR MALE GODS TO TAKE GIANTESSES AS WIVES; MUCH LESS SO FOR A GODDESS TO WED A JOTUNN.

Gefjun was an agricultural goddess who had four sons fathered by a giant. This was very unusual; male gods took wives from among the Jotnar, but the idea that a giant might marry a goddess was unacceptable – at least according to some of the tales. However, Gefjun is recorded as being able to turn her sons into oxen, which allowed her to get a lot out of a bargain with Gylfi, King of Sweden. He offered her as much land as four oxen could plough in a single day, and no doubt regretted this when her supernatural oxen-sons dragged away enough land to form the huge island of Zealand off the coast of Denmark.

BELOW: **Gefjun was able to turn her four sons into oxen to draw her plough. As children of a giant and a goddess, they were mighty labourers as King Gylfi found out to his cost.**

## The Vanir

The Vanir were supposedly equal with the Aesir, but generally had a subordinate or supportive role in the 'marriage' between the two tribes of gods. The Vanir were associated with nature,

fertility and magic, and were often more subtle than the Aesir. Their home was Vanaheim, whose location is somewhat vague, although presumably it was close to Asgard in the upper reaches of Yggdrasil. The very existence of the Vanir as such is open to some discussion; there are few references in the original sources, and it is possible that the existence of the Vanir tribe was inferred at a later date.

At risk of excessive generalization, the Vanir seem to have a role similar to that of the wife in a traditional Norse household. Women could and did own property and be independently wealthy, but most commonly made a partnership with a man in which both had distinct roles. While the husband was the obvious 'head of the household', speaking (and fighting, when necessary) for his family, the wife kept it functioning. It has been suggested that the husband was in charge of everything outside his house, but the wife was in charge of everything within it. Since a man had to live in that house, who was actually in charge in a traditional Norse marriage is open to some interpretation. The Vanir, similarly, may have wielded a great deal of influence over how and where the Aesir brought their less subtle power to bear.

## Njord and Nerthus

Njord was the father of Freya and Freyr; it is not clear who their mother might have been. Njord was one of the foremost Vanir, and was chosen to become a member of the Aesir tribe when hostages were swapped at the end of the Aesir–Vanir war. Like many of the Vanir, Njord was associated with fertility, but he was also a sea deity and a patron of wealth.

Few legends survive of Njord's deeds. It seems that he was originally of great importance in the Norse pantheon, but was

ABOVE: Njord was associated with the bounty of the sea, obtained by fishing and sea-borne trade. He was the father of Freya and Freyr. The goddess Nerthus may have been a twinned female aspect of Njord.

later eclipsed by other gods. He does feature prominently in one tale, in which he marries the female Jotunn Skadi, although his role is rather passive. Skadi was the daughter of the giant Thjazi, who had connived to kidnap the goddess Idun and her magical fruits. This resulted in his death, for which Skadi wanted revenge.

Skadi was a formidable individual, noted for her prowess at hunting, and took the direct approach. She presented herself to the gods and stated her intention to seek vengeance. This could have been a lengthy business; several of the gods had a hand in the death of Thjazi. For whatever reasons, the gods decided not to fight Skadi, but instead made peace with her. Odin cast the eyes of Thjazi into the heavens where they became stars, after which the gods tried to make Skadi laugh. If they failed, there would be no peace, yet the gods could not amuse Skadi sufficiently to sway her from

## NJORD MARRIED THE GIANTESS SKADI, DAUGHTER OF THJAZI, AS PART OF A PEACE SETTLEMENT.

RIGHT: The marriage of Skadi and Njord was ill-fated and did not last long due to their very different natures. It broke up amicably without resumption of hostility towards Asgard on Skadi's part.

her intended vengeance. Loki finally managed it in typically bizarre fashion. He tied his testicles to a goat and held a tug-of-war with it. His screams of pain – and no doubt the cries of the frightened goat – eventually caused Skadi to laugh.

Finally, the deal required that Skadi marry a god of her choice. It was not uncommon for a male god to marry a female Jotunn, but to allow a Jotunn to choose their partner was highly unusual. However, the gods went ahead on the condition that Skadi choose her husband by looking only at his legs and feet. She chose Njord, although she thought he was Baldr.

The gods gave Skadi and Njord a fine wedding, and afterwards they went to her mountaintop home, Thrymheim. Njord hated it there, finding the mountains cold and dismal, so after nine nights the couple moved to Njord's home by the sea. This was not to the liking of Skadi, who hated the noise and bustle. Skadi went home without her new husband, but (presumably since the gods had kept their end of the bargain) she made no more attempts at vengeance.

The goddess Nerthus appears to be a female form of Njord. There is linguistic evidence to indicate that the two are either male and female aspects of the same god, or a pair of matched gods. Nerthus is inferred by some sources to be the mother of

ABOVE: Nerthus' priests moved from one settlement to the next in a sort of roving religious festival. Their arrival was celebrated with feasting and a truce between enemies, which was intended to bring good fortune and plentiful harvests.

Freyr and Freya, and also to be Njord's sister. Be that as it may, Nerthus is associated with times of plenty. She, or her priests, would travel from one settlement to the next in a chariot pulled by cows, and wherever the chariot stopped there would be feasting and a period of peace.

## Freya

The daughter of Njord, Freya is often confused with Odin's wife Frigg. This is largely because the two were originally the same proto-Germanic goddess, given different but confusingly similar names and identities. Freya is married to a god named Odr, who has the same abilities as Odin and is essentially the same god.

Freya was a Vanir but joined the Aesir after the Aesir–Vanir war. She is associated with love and fertility, and was accused of sleeping with all of the gods and the Elves as well. This came from Loki, so it is possible that it was pure invention, but given Freya's characteristics there was probably at least some substance to the accusation. The Norse gods – even those not associated with love and fertility – were not known for their fidelity.

Freya had two important functions in the Norse pantheon. She was the ruler of Folkvangr, an equivalent to Valhol, where half of the great warriors slain in battle spent their afterlife. The other half were ruled by Odin, although Folkvangr and Valhol seem to have been more or less the same in many accounts.

Freya also practiced Seidr, magic connected mainly with divining and manipulating fate. She is credited with being the first of the gods to practice this form of magic, and thus of enabling mortals to learn it.

## Freyr

Freyr was the son of Njord, brother to Freya, and like her he was sent to the Aesir after the end of their conflict with the Vanir. He was a god of fertility, associated with prosperity, good harvests and families, and was often the subject of sacrifices at weddings

ABOVE: Freya was a goddess of fertility and love who nevertheless presided over half of the warriors chosen to fight at Ragnarok. She was accused of promiscuity by Loki, possibly with some basis in truth.

and other
joyous occasions. He
is sometimes referred to as
being 'hated by none', and
was apparently loved by
many – his partners included
both goddesses and Jotnar,
and allegedly his sister Freya.

Freyr, unusually, dwelt
neither in the land of the
Aesir nor the Vanir. His
home was in Alfheim, and
there are implications that
he was its ruler. How this
came to be, and what his
relationship with the Light Elves
who lived there might have been,
is not clear. Despite his generally
agreeable and benevolent nature, Freyr was
a skilled warrior. He was fated to battle the
great Fire Jotunn Surt, resulting in the death of both.

Like many of the gods, Freyr possessed magical treasures.
These included the ship *Skidbladnir*, which could be folded up
and carried in a bag. Freyr also had a chariot pulled by giant
boars, an animal with which he was closely associated – many of
the sacrifices made to him took the form of a boar.

LEFT: Freyr may have
been the ruler of
Alfheim, though his
relationship with the
Elves who lived there
remains vague. He was
fated to be killed by Surt
at Ragnarok, but not
before stabbing the fire
giants' leader in the face.

# Loki

Loki was something of a special case in Norse mythology. He was a Jotunn who was adopted by Odin as blood brother. This made him one of the Aesir, but still an outsider, which was both useful and a liability for the gods. His father was Farbauti, a Jotunn, and his mother, Laufey, is often assumed to be one as well. However, the sources are not clear on whether this is the case.

Loki was often the only one who could fix a difficult situation, since he could twist or break a deal that the other gods would be bound by, but he was also the instigator of many of the troubles that beset the gods. It was Loki that caused the chain of events that led to Idun being kidnapped by the Jotunn Thjazi. Indeed, Loki facilitated the kidnapping in return for his own survival. It was also he that rescued Idun and led Thjazi to his death.

Loki was the only Norse god whose nature changed over time. The others were many-faceted, but always the same. Even

BELOW: A carved representation of Loki. Despite his troublesome nature, Loki was at times invaluable to the gods and was a companion on many of their adventures. He caused as many problems as he solved, however.

Odin, cunning and devious as he was, remained true to his own nature. Loki, on the other hand, went from being a playful and irresponsible trickster to a vengeful enemy who led the Jotnar to storm Asgard. In the tales of his earlier adventures, Loki was a companion of the other gods. He caused trouble, but also helped out in ways that nobody else could. His deeds were often irresponsible and at times pointlessly malicious, but in a limited way. He was part of the Aesir tribe and loyal to it, although he was also wayward and unpredictable.

Later, however, Loki's pranks became increasingly nasty. His second-hand murder of Baldr was arguably just a wicked prank. The gods were amused by Baldr's invulnerability and liked to throw weapons at him as a game. From Loki's viewpoint they were just asking for something to go awry; he merely facilitated it by making a weapon from the only thing in creation that could harm Baldr and giving it to the only god (blind Hod) who would not recognize it for what it was.

Causing the death of Baldr was a prank that went too far, but a prank nonetheless. However, what Loki did next was simply malicious. Baldr could have been returned from the realm of Hel if Loki had not intervened. It was agreed that if everyone in the world wept for Baldr then he would be freed. The only creature that would not – and thus ensured Baldr's permanent death – turned out to be Loki in disguise. The implication is that even the Jotnar were willing to weep for Baldr … but not Loki, who was ostensibly a member of his own tribe.

## Is Loki the Personification of Evil?

It is not appropriate to think of Loki as 'evil' in the sense applied by monotheistic religions. His actions are self-centred, at times malicious and often detrimental to the wellbeing of others, but Loki is not 'evil' for the sake of doing bad things. He is a trickster, an outsider who does not quite fit within society, and a self-centred one at that. His actions make sense from his own perspective, just as those of Odin or Heimdall make sense from theirs.

The myths of the Norse gods are not a triumph of good gods over the evil traitor Loki, they are far more complex than that. Better to consider these as tales of a dysfunctional family riven by a feud, in which there are many agendas and in which each god acts according to his or her own nature. At times it suits the purposes of the gods to have Loki betray someone on their behalf, and of course he is not the only one to be in conflict with at least some of the gods. Arguably, the Aesir cheated the Vanir in their hostage swap, and in response the Vanir murdered Mimir by beheading him. These cannot be considered good deeds, even though they were perpetrated by the ostensible heroes of the tales.

This betrayal was too much to bear, and Loki was punished savagely. He was chained in a cave, where venom from a serpent dripped onto his face and burned him. His wife Sigyn tried to protect him by catching the venom in a bowl, but she had to empty it from time to time, leaving Loki unprotected. His shudders as the venom burned him were said to be the cause of earthquakes. He eventually escaped from the cave to seek his vengeance by bringing about Ragnarok, where he and Heimdall slew one another.

Little is known about Loki's wife, Sigyn, other than the fact that she was quite devoted to her husband – sufficiently so to spend long ages alone in a cave with him, trying to protect him from the consequences of his actions. She may or may not have been the mother of some of the monsters Loki fathered. These included the gigantic serpent Jormangandr and the great wolf Fenrir. Loki also had more normal children, such as Vali (confusingly, this is not the same Vali who avenged Baldr's death) who was turned into a wolf by the gods, and the goddess Hel. Loki was also the mother (by means of a very convoluted story recounted elsewhere) of Odin's horse Sleipnir.

## WITHOUT LOKI, THE CYCLE OF CREATION, LIFE AND DESTRUCTION COULD NOT BE COMPLETED.

Loki fulfilled an important function in Norse mythology. He was the outsider within society who could bend or ignore laws and oaths to get the gods out of trouble. He was highly useful in solving problems, but often he was the cause of those problems. He was the father of many of the monsters that the gods battled and also responsible for obtaining many of their magical treasures, giving them enemies to fight and the means to defeat them. And finally, he is the great enemy that provides a fitting finale to the tale of the Norse gods. Without Loki, the cycle of creation, life and destruction could not be completed, and the gods would be diminished for lack of a suitable challenge.

### The War Between the Gods and the Mead of Poetry

The two tribes of gods, the Aesir and the Vanir, originally were separate but were not in conflict. That changed due to the

selfishness of many among the Aesir. Freya, calling herself Heidr, arrived in Asgard and offered to work her magic for the Aesir. This was common among practitioners of the Seidr, who were often itinerant.

Freya used her magic as requested, and the Aesir were tempted by this new power into using it for selfish ends. This was a betrayal of their nature, as honourable gods and devoted kinfolk, and resentment grew among the Aesir for one another and also for what they were becoming. Rather than blame themselves for their weakness, the Aesir decided that Freya was at fault, and resolved to kill her. This proved more difficult than expected: three times Freya was burned to death, and each time she returned to life.

This treatment of their kin-goddess angered the Vanir, and escalating tensions eventually led to war between the two tribes of gods. The might of the warlike Aesir was met with the magic of the Vanir, although apparently the Vanir at times gave as good as they got in combat. They succeeded in levelling the walls of Asgard, but eventually both sides grew tired of the fighting.

A solution was proposed, by which hostages would be exchanged between the tribes. Njord, Freya and Freyr went to live among the Aesir, despite the fact that it was Freya's time with the Aesir that had started the whole conflict. However, the arrangement seems to have worked in the end; the Aesir treated their hostages well and adopted them as family.

The Vanir got Hoenir, who was very handsome, and Mimir, who was wise. This, too, seemed like a good deal and soon the Vanir had elevated Hoenir from hostage to chieftain. His decisions were good and at first everyone was happy, until the Vanir noticed that Hoenir was totally dependent on the advice of Mimir. When Mimir counselled him, Hoenir made wise decisions; when Mimir was not available Hoenir made no decisions at all.

The Vanir were angered by what they saw as a deception on the part of the Aesir. Following the precedent set with Freya, they decided to show it through the rather graphic means of murder. Mimir was decapitated and his head sent back to the Aesir. Odin managed to preserve the head with herbs and charms, permitting Mimir to serve him as an advisor thereafter. Hoenir escaped retribution and continued to live among the Vanir.

Despite this rather extreme form of diplomatic protest, the Aesir–Vanir war was not renewed. Instead, the two groups of gods reached a new agreement. The Aesir came off best in the negotiations, essentially becoming senior partners in a joint

OPPOSITE: **The war between the Aesir and the Vanir was so destructive that even the warlike Aesir wearied of it. The subsequent peace settlement favoured the Aesir more than their supposed equals, the Vanir.**

ESCALATING TENSIONS LED TO WAR BETWEEN THE AESIR AND THE VANIR.

tribe of gods. The deal was sealed in the traditional manner of spitting into a vessel, wherein they jointly formed a new being called Kvasir. Despite being made from spit, Kvasir's name meant 'fermented berry juice' and he was the wisest of all things.

Kvasir went out into the world dispensing wisdom to anyone who needed it, which eventually brought him to the home of the dwarfs Fjalar and Galar. They murdered Kvasir and used his blood to make mead, which contained his vast wisdom. This was the Mead of Poetry, and it made whoever drank it wise enough to become a scholar or bard.

The mead apparently did not make the Dwarfs very wise. Although they escaped retribution for a time by claiming that Kvasir's great wisdom had somehow choked him to death, they attracted attention by becoming serial killers. First they drowned the Jotunn Gilling, apparently just for the sake of it,

RIGHT: Illustrations such as this plate from an early twentieth-century version of the Norse tales have shaped our modern perception of the gods of Asgard. The gods might have been very differently imagined by a ninth-century Norseman.

then they murdered his wife because the sound of her grief was irritating. Their weapon of choice was a millstone dropped on the giantess' head.

The Jotunn Suttung, son of Gilling, deduced that the Dwarfs had murdered his parents and went to take vengeance. However, he was dissuaded when the Dwarfs offered him the three vats of mead they had brewed. He gave the mead to his daughter Gunnlod to protect.

Odin heard of the mead and decided to obtain its wisdom. To do so he decided to enlist the help of Baugi, brother of Suttung. There was little prospect of this being offered freely, so Odin resorted to trickery. First he deceived the nine servants of Baugi into accidentally killing one another with their scythes, then presented himself to Baugi as an itinerant labourer who could do the work of nine men. Suddenly finding himself in need of such an individual, Baugi hired the disguised Odin, who made good on his promise and did nine men's work for the whole season.

Baugi then had to keep his end of their bargain and help Odin get the mead. He showed Odin the nearest place to the dwelling of Suttung and drilled a hole through the mountainside for him. Odin turned himself into a snake and slithered inside before transforming himself into a young man. In this guise he seduced Gunnlod, sleeping with her for three nights in return for a single drink of the mead for each night. Odin's three sips turned out to be vast gulps in which he downed the entire contents of the three vats.

ABOVE: A medieval representation of Baugi drilling a hole into the mountainside to grant Odin access to the abode of Suttung and the Mead of Poetry therein. The manner of dress is, of course, anachronistic.

Odin then turned himself into an eagle to escape, and despite the pursuit of Suttung (also in the form of an eagle) he managed to reach Asgard where he regurgitated the mead into new containers. Some of it dripped from his beak while he was an eagle, and fell to Midgard where it inspired human poets and scholars. Thus the existence of skalds, bards and lawspeakers in Midgard can be tracked back to the mystical conflict between the two tribes of gods.

## The Treasures of the Gods

The Norse gods obtained most of their treasures as a result of Loki's pranks. To put that another way, Loki obtained treasures for the gods as a means of saving his own skin after doing something that angered his peers. Most of the treasures resulted, directly or indirectly, from an incident where Loki decided to cut off the beautiful golden hair of Thor's wife Sif. It is not altogether clear why he thought this was a good idea and how he expected to get away with it, but Loki was never one to care much about the consequences of his actions.

Thor was very prone to boasting, and no doubt got on Loki's nerves from time to time. It may be that Loki cut off Sif's hair when she was sleeping to pay Thor back for bragging about how wonderful his wife's hair was. Whatever the reason, Thor was naturally very angry when he saw what Loki had done, and swore vengeance. Faced with the alternatives of finding a way to replace Sif's hair or being beaten to a pulp by Thor, Loki journeyed to Nidavellir (or Svartalfheim – the names are used interchangeably in some versions of the tale), the land of the Dwarfs. There, he persuaded the two sons of Ivaldi to help him.

THOR SWORE VENGEANCE ON LOKI FOR CUTTING OFF HIS WIFE SIF'S HAIR.

The sons of Ivaldi created magical golden hair that would grow naturally once Sif wore it, and in addition made the ship *Skidbladnir*, which could transport all the gods yet be folded up and carried in a bag. The ship was to be given to Freyr, while for Odin they made the spear Gungnir, which never missed its target.

Loki was impressed and declared the two Dwarfs to be the

LEFT: Dwarf craftsmen were able to make all manner of magical treasures, so it was to them that Loki turned when he needed a replacement for Sif's golden hair. The gods did very well out of this escapade, gaining several other magical treasures.

cleverest smiths in creation. Whether or not he deliberately did so where other Dwarf smiths would hear, or simply took advantage of what happened next, the Dwarf brothers Brokk and Eitri (Sindri in some versions) did indeed overhear. Naturally they disputed the assertion, and said they could make three items that were better than those Loki already had. A bet was agreed, with the loser to forfeit his head.

Eitri went to his forge and began work, with Brokk working the bellows. Loki naturally tried to disrupt their efforts, turning himself into a fly that pestered and bit Brokk. Despite this, Brokk stayed true to his task and enabled Eitri to produce two wonderful treasures. For Freyr there was the golden boar Gullin-Borsti, and for Odin he created the magical arm ring Draupnir, which would create eight additional rings each ninth night.

Loki was in danger of losing the bet, and therefore also his head, and redoubled his efforts to distract Brokk. He stung the Dwarf close to his eye, forcing him to cease pumping the bellows for a moment while he wiped away the blood. This was enough to cause Eitri's work to go awry. The Dwarf had been making a hammer for Thor, named Mjolnir. Although it was still magical, the handle came out much shorter than intended.

## ONCE AGAIN, LOKI MANAGED TO AVOID HIS FATE BY TWISTING THE WORDS OF THE BET HE HAD MADE.

The two Dwarfs went to Asgard with Loki. They presented their gifts to the gods, who decided that Brokk and Eitri had indeed made better treasures than the sons of Ivaldi. Loki had lost his bet, and Brokk was entitled to cut off his head. Loki fled for his life, but was chased down by Thor who returned him to face justice. Even then, Loki was able to weasel out of his fate. He pointed out that while he had wagered his head, Brokk was not entitled to his neck and so could not cut it. The gods agreed to this, but Brokk countered by saying that if Loki's head was his, he could at least sew his mouth shut. He did so, and left Asgard.

### Odin's Treasures

In some versions of the Norse tales, the spear Gungnir was made for Odin when Loki went to find a replacement for Sif's hair. Other versions state that the spear was already made and Loki asked for it as an additional gift for the gods. Either way, Gungnir, whose name means Swaying One, is said to be fashioned from ash wood from the world-tree Yggdrasil. Odin added his own magic to Gungnir in the form of runes he inscribed upon the shaft.

Gungnir was so well made that it could not miss its target, even in the hands of an unskilled user. It may or may not have been the spear that Odin threw at the beginning of the Aesir–Vanir war; that spear is not recorded as hitting anyone, but travelling right over the Vanir army. This deed became a tradition: a spear cast at the beginning of a battle was a way of determining if a battle would go well.

Odin's magical arm-ring Draupnir was made by the Dwarfs, and would drop eight copies of itself each ninth night. This valuable item was placed on Baldr's body at his funeral, a practice reflected in the use of grave-goods by Norse people.

## Thor's Treasures

The hammer Mjolnir (which translates as 'Lightning') became very much a symbol of Thor despite being defective. This was presented as an advantage – Mjolnir could be wielded in one hand and concealed about Thor's person. If hurled, it would not miss and would never go so far that it could not be recovered. In some versions of Thor's adventures, Mjolnir magically returns to his hand even if lying on the ground after striking someone, and enables him to fly by throwing his weapon and being dragged along behind it. The details are typically left rather vague; this is probably not a very dignified way to get about.

Mjolnir required enormous strength to wield. Even Thor required magical assistance in the form of his iron gauntlets Jarngreipr and a belt called Meginjord that increased his strength. With this assistance Thor could destroy almost anything by smiting it with his hammer, although there are instances in the tales of his adventures where he failed.

Thor also had a magical chariot pulled by goats named Tanngrisnir and Tanngnjostr, which could be killed and eaten each night. So long as the bones were left in the goats' skins overnight, they would be brought back to life the next day. One of the goats became lame after Thor used them to feed himself and a family of farmers he found hospitality with. During the night one of the family, still hungry, broke a leg bone to get at the marrow and permanently made the goat lame. Thor took the perpetrator and his sister as his servants as punishment.

ABOVE: Amulets and other items in the shape of a hammer symbolized Thor and also the Norse religion in general. Even after the coming of Christianity a hammer/cross amulet was worn by many Norsemen.

## Freya's Treasures

The goddess Freya possessed a chariot pulled by cats, which are typically portrayed as grey or black. It has been suggested that this is a subtle reference to Freya's great powers of influence – anyone who can get cats to go in the same direction long enough to pull a chariot is persuasive indeed! Be that as it may, Freya had other means of transport, too.

Freya sometimes rode the magical boar Hildisvini, who was said to be her human lover in disguise. She also possessed a cloak of falcon feathers that enabled the wearer to fly between worlds. This cloak was borrowed on several occasions by other gods.

Freya's greatest treasure, certainly the one that caused the most trouble, was the necklace Brisingamen. She obtained this when she chanced upon four Dwarf craftsmen making it in a cave. Being fond of beautiful things, she naturally wanted it. The Dwarfs refused all offers of gold, but agreed to hand over the necklace if Freya spent the night with each of them. She did so, but was seen by Loki who immediately went to Odin and told him what Freya was doing.

Odin was angry, although it is interesting to recall that he was married to Frigg, not Freya. This seems to be one of several occasions where Frigg and Freya are confused in the Norse myths. Be that as it may, Odin sent Loki to get the necklace from Freya, which he did while she was sleeping. He did not take it to Odin, however. Freya then went to Odin, distraught at the loss of her precious possession, and asked for his help in retrieving it. Angry now at Loki as well as Freya, Odin agreed on condition that Freya caused a war in Midgard.

BELOW: Freya could travel by chariot or ride her magical boar. She seems to have loaned out her cloak of falcon feathers more often than using it; the cloak features in several tales where gods must reach other worlds quickly.

LEFT: Freya's necklace Brisingamen seems to have caused no end of trouble for all concerned. It is notable that Heimdall, Loki's enemy, was sent to chase him down when he stole it and fled in the form of a seal.

Once this was done, Odin sent Heimdall, who had no love for Loki, to pursue him. Loki had turned himself into a seal, so Heimdall did likewise and confronted him. On this occasion, Heimdall was victorious and brought Loki – along with the necklace – back to Asgard.

## Other Treasures

Heimdall, guardian of the Bifrost bridge, had a horn named Gjallar or Gjallarhorn, and was armed with a sword named

# Norse Word Play

Much of the confusion surrounding the Norse mythos arises from the use of 'kennings'. These are colourful words or phrases used to replace a simpler one and while they do add to the drama and literary richness of the tales, they can also confuse matters.

Some kennings are straightforward, such as 'sea-steed' for ship. Others are less so. For example a man who is 'the enemy of gold' is generous or not greedy. Some are downright perplexing. For example Greip is the name of a specific female giant. In the tale of how Thjazi kidnapped Idun, he is described using a kenning as the son of the suitor of Greip, which can be taken to mean that he is related to Greip. This is probably not so; more likely this is a complex kenning in which Greip is a generic term for any female giant, making the 'suitor of Greip' a non-specific male giant. Thus the kenning is a roundabout way of stating that Thjazi was a giant and nothing more.

This sort of literary obfuscation creates confusion about who or what is the subject of a tale, and can result in doubt about whether – for example – a given hero or god had a sword that was actually called ben-grefil ('wound-hoe') or whether this was just a kenning for 'sword'.

Hofud. Loki, who Heimdall fought to their mutual death, had a sword named Laevateinn, although this may be a kenning simply meaning 'sword'. The same name is given to other weapons in various tales. A number of magical swords were also wielded by mortals in the sagas, and some versions of the tales associate these weapons with those wielded by the gods.

Other parallels exist. In addition to Draupnir, another golden ring that made copies of itself existed. This was Andvarinaut, and unlike Draupnir, it was cursed. It was originally owned by the Dwarf Andvari, who was tricked out of it by Loki and placed a curse on the ring in revenge. Loki then passed the ring to others, causing chaos by doing so. The Dwarf Fafnir murdered his father (the Dwarf King Hreidmar) to get the ring and was subsequently turned into a dragon to guard it. Although not named as such, Andvarinaut is the ring in Wagner's *Der Ring Des Nibelungen*.

Some magical items were not treasures so much as solutions to a problem. The magical rope or chain Gleipnir was one such device. The gods had decided that they needed to bind the monstrous wolf Fenrir, but no ordinary chain would suffice. So they had the Dwarf craftsmen make them a magical cord from mystical materials. These included the sound of a cat's footfall, the beard of a woman, the roots of a mountain, the sinews of a bear, spittle from a bird and the breath of a fish. The cord Gleipnir (which translates as 'deceiver') was capable of binding anyone or anything, and held Fenrir until finally, as the day of

Ragnarok neared, he broke free to seek vengeance upon those that bound him.

Many other magical 'treasures' were actually living creatures or the remnants of them. The head of Mimir counselled Odin; mystical animals provided sustenance to warriors at Valhol and replenished the magical wells by the roots of Yggdrasil. These creatures and beings provided benefits as great as any of the inanimate items used by the gods and can be considered to be among the magical treasures of the mythical Norse cosmos.

LEFT: The Rhinemaidens of Wagner's 'Ring Cycle' are not part of the Norse mythos, but have become associated with it as a result of the operas. They originated in Germanic myths such as the *Niebelunglied*.

# 3

# JOTNAR

Norse mythology was populated by a range of creatures in addition to mortals and gods. Some were monsters, some appear to be personifications of natural forces and some were powerful supernatural beings. Others, like the Jotnar, were very similar to the gods and could have children with them. Indeed, many of the gods had at least one parent who was a Jotunn, and the dividing line between Jotunn and god seems to be at times spiritual or social rather than being based upon parentage.

Someone who was accepted as a member of the Aesir or Vanir tribe was a god, regardless of parentage. Thus, despite being fully Jotunn, Loki was considered to be a god-by-adoption. Arguably he reverted to being a Jotunn after (or during) his imprisonment in the cave after slaying Baldr. However, Loki is generally considered to be a god whereas some other giants who performed roles normally associated with gods are still referred to as Jotunn.

It is notable that where this occurs, the giant's role is connected with the natural world and natural forces rather than people. For example, Ran and Aegir are Jotnar, and are

OPPOSITE: The great wolf Fenrir was a child of Loki and a giantess named Angrboda. Fenrir was so powerful and ferocious that the gods considered it necessary to bind him using a magical cord named Gleipnir.

associated with the sea. The Vanir god Njord is associated with seafaring, i.e. human activity at sea. Thus the Jotnar represent the natural world and the gods are associated with what people do in that world. The Jotnar were generally blamed for nature's destructive power – high winds, thick mist and other difficult conditions were the fault of the Jotnar, whose sneezes could cause earthquakes.

RIGHT: In Wagner's *Der Ring Des Nibelungen,* the giants Fafner and Fasolt quarrel over the division of gold, including the cursed ring of the title. Fasolt is clubbed to death and Fafner is turned into a dragon to guard the hoard.

# The Jotnar

Although the word Jotunn (plural Jotnar) is generally translated as 'Giant', the term means something closer to 'Devourer' which suggests that these were inimical and destructive creatures. However, some Jotunn seem to have got along well with the gods well enough to marry into their tribes and produce godly children. Others seem fairly peaceable, or at least have no recorded conflicts with the Aesir or the Vanir.

There were two types of giant associated with fire and cold. The Hrimthursar, or Frost Giants, originated in Niflheim, although many later made their homes in Jotunheim. The frost giants were generally associated with ice, cold and remote places although some seem to have lived in more hospitable lands. The Eldjotnar, or fire giants, came from Muspelheim and are sometimes referred to as Muspelsmegir, or 'sons of Muspelheim'.

The Jotnar varied considerably in appearance. Some were handsome or beautiful, sufficiently so to make them desirable as wives (or, in rare cases, husbands) for the gods. Others were huge or malformed, and some were outright monsters. Creatures such as the serpent Jormungand and the nine-headed Thrivaldi bore little resemblance to more normal-appearing Jotunn, such as Ran or even Surt, but they all belonged to the same group. It is not appropriate to try to think of the Jotnar as a race or species. They were alike in origins and general nature – a mystical grouping rather than a family or race in the conventional earthly sense.

## IDENTIFYING THE JOTNAR

Distinctions between the various types of Jotnar are vague at times. It is frequently unclear what kind of Jotunn is being referred to in a given passage, and often it does not really matter. Rather than a simple fire/frost giant distinction based upon origins, the Jotnar are perhaps better grouped according to their relations with the gods and which tales they appear in. In some cases their nature dictates the form of these interactions – for example, Jotnar identified as fire giants seem always to be inimical to the gods.

In later Norse/Scandinavian mythology the term 'troll' is used more or less interchangeably with Jotunn or giant, whereas in Anglo-Saxon tales the word 'Etin' is used. Variations also exist upon names, partly due to Anglicization and partly because there was no written form of the Norse tales until centuries after they had been supplanted by Christian beliefs.

ABOVE: **The term 'troll' originally applied to the Jotnar. After the coming of Christianity, the trolls of legend gradually took on their own identity as powerful, but often dimwitted creatures.**

## The Primordial Jotnar

Some Jotnar appear only in tales of the creation of the cosmos and the early events thereafter. The majority of these beings were killed during or after the battle between Odin and his brothers and the primordial giant Ymir.

## Ymir

Ymir was the first of the Jotnar. In fact, Ymir may be the first of all beings, although the tale of Surt the Fire Giant seems to suggest that he existed even before Ymir. Be that as it may, Ymir came to be as a result of the meeting of fire and ice in the Ginnungagap, in which all possibility lay in a well of magic and energy. Ymir was the parent of many Jotnar, although most were killed when Odin and his brothers slew Ymir and used his body to make the world. His offspring included giantesses who became wives to the first gods, although the Aesir themselves were descended from a man licked out of the ice by Ymir's cow Audhumbla. The first Dwarfs came from maggots found in Ymir's corpse, and arguably since the world – including its trees – were made from Ymir's flesh and hair, and the gods then made humans out of the trees, Ymir is also the distant progenitor of humanity.

BELOW: The magical cow Audhumbla provided sustenance for the primordial giant Ymir whilst licking the ice for sustenance. As the ice was licked away it revealed Búri, first of the Aesir.

## Bestla and Her Brother

Bestla was a giantess, apparently the daughter of a Jotunn named Bolthorn who was one of the earliest offspring of Ymir. Bestla married Bor, son of the first of the Aesir, and had three sons named Odin, Vili and Ve. Bestla had a brother, who is not named in the only tale in which he is mentioned. This unknown uncle taught Odin his nine magic songs; in traditional Norse society it was often an uncle or a friend of his father that would teach a young man how to handle weapons. Magic was more commonly considered the province of women, but the role of uncle as tutor was certainly in keeping with traditional values. It has been suggested that this mysterious uncle may have been Mimir, who is sometimes referred to as a god and sometimes as a Jotunn. If Odin's uncle was indeed Mimir, then he was a Jotunn who was adopted into the Aesir tribe as a god, then traded as a hostage to the Vanir who murdered him. Receiving his head would have been grievous to Odin, yet the Vanir–Aesir war was not resumed.

ABOVE: Most of the Jotnar seem to have been able to tolerate sunlight quite happily and lived on the surface. Some, however, shared a trait in common with some of the Dwarfs: they could be turned to stone by sunlight.

## Bergelmir and his Wife

Bergelmir was the son of Thrudgelmir, who was in turn the son of a giant named Aurgelmir. This seems to be an alternate name for Ymir, making Bergelmir one of the earliest of the Jotnar. Along with his wife, he survived the tide of blood that followed the slaying of Ymir. Accounts of how this happened vary.

In some versions of the tale Bergelmir was a full-grown Jotunn, in others a small child. His conveyance has been variously described as a cradle, a hollowed-out log or a box or chest. The tale of Bergelmir and his wife was clearly distorted by the chronicler's familiarity with the Christian story of the Great Flood, resulting in an attempt to turn Bergelmir into a Noah-like figure whereas the original tale may have been quite different.

Be that as it may, Bergelmir and his wife were carried far away by the flood that killed all of the other Hrimthursar. Once they reached their new home they bred a whole new race of Jotnar.

Thrudgelmir, who may well have been the six-headed Jotnar formed from the mating of Ymir's legs (or feet, depending on the version of the tale), perished when his parent was slain by drowning in the tide of Ymir's blood.

MUSPELHEIM WAS THE HOME OF THE ELDJOTNAR, OR FIRE GIANTS, WHO WERE HOSTILE TO THE GODS AND PLOTTED THEIR DESTRUCTION.

## The Fire Giants (Eldjotnar)

Few Jotunn are specifically identified as being fire giants, which could be taken to mean that most of those encountered by the gods are descendants of the original frost giants, while the Eldjotnar lurk in Muspelheim waiting for a chance to march out and destroy the world and have few interactions with the gods before that.

Alternatively, it may be that some fire giants relocated to Jotunheim and that the distinction between fire and frost Jotnar ceased to matter so much after a while. The Jotunn Aegir, who lived in Asgard and was friendly with the gods, is in some sources claimed to be the son of Fornjot who is a fire giant. If so, fire giants were not always inimical to the gods (although some individuals were), in much the same way that many frost giants were willing to have friendly or at least neutral relations with the gods.

## Surt

Surt was the lord of Muspelheim and leader of the Eldjotnar, or Fire Giants. His name is usually translated to mean 'black' in keeping with his charred appearance. The origins of Surt are not clear; Muspelheim was the first land of the Norse cosmos, predating Niflheim, and it may be that Surt was always there. Once the children of Ymir appeared, Surt and his fire giants interacted with them, but seem to have a different, obscure origin.

Muspelheim is said to be impassable to those not native to it, but all the same Surt guarded its borders against incursions until it was time to attack Asgard at Ragnarok. He was armed with a flaming sword, with which he slew Freyr and set fire to Asgard and even Yggdrasil. It was Surt's fire that burned the world and completed its destruction.

It has been suggested that Surt is the reason Muspelheim was a fiery land – he made it that way with his sword. This in turn suggests that Surt was even older that Ymir; he was present at the beginning of the cosmos and at the end. He is, not surprisingly, associated with volcanoes. The Norsemen who settled in Iceland would have been reminded about the power of Surt from time to time by eruptions and plumes of smoke from the mountains. Surt remains influential to this day – when a new Icelandic island emerged from the sea as a result of volcanic action between 1963 and 1967 it was naturally named Surtsey.

Surt apparently had a wife named Sinmara. The evidence for her is scanty, and comes mainly from a passage whose meaning is unclear unless interpreted as a name. Sinmara is noted as being

ABOVE: **The fire giant Surt set the world aflame at Ragnarok and ultimately caused its destruction. It is notable that he fought Freyr, who was associated with fertility and life rather than Odin, chief of the gods.**

the guardian of a weapon named Lævateinn, although this could be a kenning for a sword, a magic staff or something else entirely.

ABOVE: Logi represented fire, and thus had an unfair advantage in an eating contest, since fire consumes everything. His opponent Loki made a credible effort but was comprehensively out-eaten by Logi.

BELOW: Odin was less than faithful to his wife Frigg, having relations with several Jotnar, including Jord, who was the mother of Thor, and Gunnlod, who guarded the Mead of Poetry.

## Logi

Logi (sometimes also referred as Halogi) was the son of the Fire Giant Fornjot. He lived at least some of the time in Utgard, the castle of Utgarda-Loki (Skrymir) in Jotunheim. There, he assisted Skrymir in deceiving Loki and Thor. Both were the subject of various challenges, and Loki was matched against Logi in an eating contest. Although Loki did his best, and matched Logi in consumption of the meat he was served, he was up against fire itself and stood no chance – Logi ate the meat at the same rate as his opponent, but he also devoured the bones and the trencher his meal was served upon. Logi was married to the giantess Glod, and together they had two daughters, Eisa and Emiyrja. The names of all the female Jotunn are associated with embers.

## Jotnar Associated with Odin

Odin was half Aesir (by way of his father Bor) and half Jotunn.

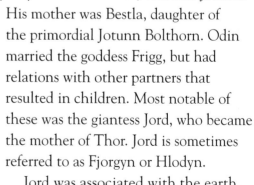

His mother was Bestla, daughter of the primordial Jotunn Bolthorn. Odin married the goddess Frigg, but had relations with other partners that resulted in children. Most notable of these was the giantess Jord, who became the mother of Thor. Jord is sometimes referred to as Fjorgyn or Hlodyn.

Jord was associated with the earth, and had a prestigious pedigree. Her father was Annar and her mother Nat (sometimes Nott), or night. Nat had three husbands, and by them she bore Jord, Dag (day) and Audr (prosperity). Jord was associated with the earth in a primal way – as a Jotunn, she personified a natural force or state, whereas the goddesses associated with the earth tended to be patrons of farming or fertility, i.e. activities associated with the earth.

Nat was the daughter of Narfi (sometimes given as Norfi), who was one of the earliest giants in existence, and the mother of Dag (day). These two beings rode in chariots pulled by magical horses, racing endlessly around the world that is personified by Jord. According to Snorri Sturluson, Nat had a third child named Audr (prosperity) but there is no other evidence of this. Audr, if he existed at all, would have been an uncle to Thor. His father is given as being a Jotunn named Naglfari.

Odin also had a child with a being named Rind. She is sometimes listed as a human and sometimes as a goddess, but was probably a Jotunn. As a Jotunn, she bore the child Vali to Odin; Vali is notable as the avenger of Baldr. There is a less pleasant version of this tale in which Rind was a human princess whom Odin raped. He was at the time seeking vengeance for the slaying of Baldr, and on the advice of seers went to see the King of the Ruthenians. There, he made advances to the King's daughter Rinda, who refused him.

Odin then used magic to make Rinda go insane, and disguised himself as a female physician or seeress named Wecha. When asked about Rinda's condition, Wecha advised her father to tie her to a bed as the cure for her madness would cause violence for a time. Odin then raped Rinda, who subsequently bore a child named Bous. Bous avenged Baldr in this version of the tale, as the seers had predicted.

# THE FAMILY OF LOKI

Loki was adopted into the Aesir tribe as a blood brother to Odin, making him a god, although his parents were – according to most sources – Jotnar. Some sources refer to members of Loki's family as gods, although this may be nothing more than the common god/giant confusion resulting from the fact that both had god-like powers.

Loki's father was Farbauti, whose name means 'cruel (or powerful, dangerous) striker'. Farbauti was associated with lightning, and Loki with wildfire. The mythic connotations of this are largely lost, but there was presumably an ancient myth in proto-Norse society of lighting striking some naturally flammable material and causing fire. That material is represented by Laufey or Nal, who were associated with leaves and pine needles respectively. Loki is referred to as the son of 'Farbauti and Laufey, or Nal', suggesting that nobody knew which was his mother rather than this being a case of conflicting stories.

Loki had two brothers, Helblindi and Byleistr, and is referred to as 'brother of Byleistr' as a kenning. This does not necessarily mean that Helblindi and Byleistr were the sons of Farbauti (or either of the two female Jotunn suspected to be Loki's mother), although this relationship is generally inferred.

## Storm Giants

Some of the Jotnar were associated with storms and bad weather, and are referred to at times as Storm Giants. Whether they originated from the fire or frost giants, or appeared later from some other source, remains unclear. Among them were Byleistr, brother to Loki, and the extremely rich Jotunn Olvaldi. The latter had three sons: Gang, Idi and Thjazi.

When Olvaldi died, his three sons found a novel way of splitting his vast fortune between them. There was so much gold that it could not be counted, so the sons took turns filling their mouths until all the gold was divided up. This gave rise to kennings referring to the speech or words of these giants as a synonym for gold or wealth.

Idi and Gang do not feature prominently in the Norse tales, but Thjazi does. He was apparently able to turn himself into an eagle and to prevent food from cooking using his magic. He used this talent to trick Loki into attacking him with a branch, and was thus able to carry the mischievous god off and extract from him a promise to help kidnap the goddess Idun and her magical fruits. The subsequent rescue led to a pursuit in which Thjazi was incinerated by the gods.

## Skadi (or Skathi)

Skadi is sometimes referred to as a goddess, and fulfils the role of a winter-god in Norse mythology. She was an excellent hunter and proficient in using skates or skis. Her father was Thjazi, and after his death she sought revenge. This led to a peace deal whereby she married the god Njord, but neither could live in the other's abode so they split up and Skadi returned to her mountain home. Relations with the gods seem to have remained amicable – some sources suggest that Skadi had children with Odin. Skadi also participated in the punishment of Loki, placing the serpent above him where its burning venom would drip onto his face.

## Asgardian Jotnar

Three of the Jotnar had homes in Asgard, which is perhaps one reason why some of them are at times referred to as gods. Of the three, Loki was in fact a god, having been adopted into the Aesir tribe as the blood brother of Odin. The others were and remained Jotnar. Karl is sometimes stated to be the brother of Loki and/or Aegir, although this is debatable. He plays a far smaller role in the Norse tales than Loki or Aegir.

## Aegir and Ran

Aegir and Ran were married giants who were closely associated with the sea. They feature in several tales of the Norse gods, and seem to have been very friendly with them. Aegir (whose name translates as 'Ocean') represented the bountiful seas that facilitated trade and provided food. He presided over great feasts at which the gods were often guests. His home was in Asgard, and perhaps for this reason he is sometimes referred to as a sea-god rather than a Jotun associated with the sea.

Ran (whose name translates as 'Plunderer') represented the dangers of the sea. She would catch seafarers in her net and drown them if she could, and as such acts as a sort of death-goddess in the Norse pantheon. Hers are the dead drowned at sea, who would not go to Helheim, Folkvang or Valhol. Ran's net was borrowed by Loki to catch the Dwarf Andvari, who could turn himself into a fish.

Aegir and Ran are sometimes referred to as being gods rather than Jotnar. They certainly fulfilled godly roles and were friends of the gods, but sources vary in their references. They had nine daughters, of whom seven were named Blodughadda, Bylgja, Dufa, Hefring, Himingglaeva, Hronn and Kolg. The other two are given different names according to various sources. They were Drofn, who was sometimes called Bara, and Ud, whose name is sometimes given as Unn.

The daughters of Ran and Aegir were associated with the waves of the sea. It has been suggested that they were the nine mothers of Heimdall. This is supported by the assertion that Heimdall was the child of nine sisters, but other sources name the nine giantesses who were his mothers, and they have different names to the children of Aegir and Ran.

BELOW: Aegir represented the bountiful oceans that provided food and transportation. He was generous and sufficiently friendly with the gods that he made his home in Asgard, a place fiercely defended against most other Jotnar.

OPPOSITE: The giantess Skadi married the god Njord as part of a peace settlement. This was highly unusual – gods often took giantesses as their wives, but seem to have been opposed to the idea of a goddess marrying a Jotunn.

ABOVE: Loki's children included the humanoid Hel, who is often considered to be a goddess rather than a Jotunn, and monsters such as Jormungand and Fenrir. Jormungand was hurled out of Asgard by Odin, whilst Fenrir was bound, albeit at great cost.

## The Children of Loki

Loki's wife was Sigyn, about whom little is known other than her obvious devotion to her husband. Together they had at least two children, Narfi and Vali, who seem to have been unremarkable among the gods. There are few references to them until the slaying of Baldr, at which point they met an unpleasant fate. Vali was exiled from Asgard, but then hunted down and captured. This parallels the custom of outlawry in traditional Norse society, which could be for a set period of time or permanent. Either way, outlaws had no protection from any law and could be killed without penalty by anyone willing to fight them.

Vali was turned into a wolf by the gods after his capture, whereupon he attacked his brother Narfi and tore him apart. Narfi's intestines were then used to bind Loki to three stones in a cave. They turned to iron once they were in place, holding Loki for many ages until he finally broke free to begin Ragnarok. Loki's wife attempted to protect him from the venom of a serpent placed above him by Skadi; it is not clear why she could not move the serpent instead.

# Hel

Hel was an ambiguous figure whose very existence in the form she was given remains debatable. According to Snorri Sturluson, she is either a Jotunn or a goddess – or perhaps both – who is the child of Loki and the Jotunn Angrboda. However, Sturluson was not above inventing details to help the mythos fit together a little more tidily.

Hel had dominion over the dead of all the Nine Worlds, and ruled a land named Helheim that is sometimes referred to as Hel. This can create confusion as to whether the goddess or her realm is the subject of a given passage, but it may be that there was no difference – the place of the dead was also the goddess of the dead.

The location of Helheim is vague. It is often depicted as being a separate realm, although many sources place it in Niflheim. Helheim, if indeed it did lie in Niflheim, was separated from the rest of the realm by a high wall. This fits with the idea that the dragon Nidhogg – who resides in Niflheim by the root of Yggdrasil – nibbled on or drank the blood from corpses. Nidhogg was only permitted to pester the corpses of the dead sent to Nastrond, the 'corpse-shore', a specific part of Helheim.

Nastrond and the torments of Nidhogg were reserved for the worst sorts of people, i.e. those who committed the crimes that most damaged Norse society. These included murder, adultery and the breaking of oaths. The idea that there was a special part of Helheim for those who committed these crimes may be a later Christian invention, in which case Nastrond, too, may be a later addition to the mythos. However, a goddess or being that may be Hel has been identified on Migration Period jewellery, so it is likely that some version of Hel existed long before the Christian scholar Sturluson wrote his Eddas.

## LOKI'S MONSTROUS OFFSPRING

Loki had children by another mother (and, in one bizarre case, was mother to a horse), the giantess Angrboda whose name can be translated as 'bringer of sorrow (or grief)'. The gods were wary of these children, fully expecting them to cause serious problems. In this expectation they were correct. The monstrous children of Angrboda and Loki were Jotunn, beings of power, and one of them was recognized as more or less a goddess. This was Hel, who was given dominion over the dead of the Nine Worlds. Hel is generally depicted as humanoid, much like the Aesir and the Vanir, whereas the other two famous children of Loki – Jormungand and Fenrir – were nothing like human. In addition to these offspring, Loki was also the father of Fenrir, the ferocious wolf that bit off Tyr's hand after he was tricked into being shackled by the gods.

ABOVE: The serpent Jormungand was perhaps the greatest of all the Norse monsters, making it a fitting enemy for the warrior god Thor. His early encounters with it were inconclusive; at Ragnarok they slew one another.

# Jormungand

Jormungand, whose name translates as 'great beast' or 'great monster', was the most monstrous of Loki's children, taking the form of a huge serpent. Odin got rid of the serpent – at least for a time – by hurling it into the sea surrounding Midgard, where it grew to such a great size that it encircled the whole world and could swallow its own tail. Thus Jormungand is also known as the Midgard Serpent or the World Serpent.

Thor had a particular enmity with the serpent, which was fated to kill him (and indeed did, although it died first). He encountered it on three occasions. On the first, Thor was challenged by the Jotunn King Utgarda-Loki to show his strength by lifting up a giant cat. Thor could not do so, although he did manage to lift it far enough to get one paw off the ground. This, Utgarda-Loki conceded, was a very impressive feat since the cat was actually Jormungand disguised by magic.

On the second occasion, Thor went fishing with the giant Hymir and managed to catch the serpent. He was prevented from killing it by Hymir, and did not encounter Jormungand again until Ragnarok.

# Fenrir

The great wolf Fenrir was the most frightening of Loki's three monstrous children. Fearing what might happen if he were banished and left to his own devices in the same manner as Hel or Jormungand, the gods decided to keep him in Asgard, where they hoped to bring him under control.

This proved to be impossible. The wolf grew rapidly and had a voracious appetite, and was not above biting at those who were trying to feed him. Soon only Tyr was brave enough to go near Fenrir, and since he was fated to slay Odin on the day of Ragnarok, something had to be done. The gods decided to bind

Fenrir, which was a risky prospect. His strength was such that he broke every chain placed upon him, to the increasing dismay of the gods who nevertheless kept trying. They prevented an angry rampage by Fenrir by convincing him the binding attempts were a game and a chance to show off his immense strength.

The denizens of the Norse world – gods, men and monsters – rarely passed up the chance for a bit of bravado, and Fenrir played along for a time. Eventually he became suspicious, especially when he was presented with a flimsy-looking cord named Gleipnir. This was made from exotic materials by the Dwarfs at the gods' request, specifically to bind Fenrir.

Correctly realizing that something was afoot, the wolf refused to be bound with this magical cord unless the gods promised to release him if he could not escape on his own. As guarantee, one of the gods must place his hand in Fenrir's mouth until he was released. Tyr was the only god brave enough for this task, knowingly sacrificing his hand to protect the cosmos from Fenrir – and perhaps as a blood-price for breaking the oath to free him. Fenrir could not break free, and bit off Tyr's hand in his rage.

BELOW: The deliberate sacrifice of Tyr's hand in return for binding the wolf Fenrir was an act of great courage on Tyr's part, and entirely in character for a brave warrior and protector of his people.

He was taken to a remote place and chained to a rock with a sword jamming his jaws open. A river of drool ran from Fenrir's mouth while he was bound, but he was unable to do more than howl in anger until Ragnarok neared, when he finally escaped. At Ragnarok he slew Odin as had been foretold, but was then struck down by Odin's son Vidar.

Fenrir is sometimes confused or associated with other wolves of the Norse mythos. He appears in only one major tale under his own name, but he may also be the wolf described as eating the sun at Ragnarok. Some stories have the wolf Skoll doing so, and he is definitely not Fenrir, but there are references to Fenrir swallowing the sun and also to a wolf named Garmr breaking his chains and eating the moon before Ragnarok. It may be that there is a mystical connection between Fenrir and these destructive wolves, or that the tales have become confused, duplicated or distorted over the centuries.

## THE CROWING OF THE ROOSTER SIGNIFIED THE ONSET OF RAGNAROK.

### The Nine Mothers of Heimdall

Heimdall was born of nine mothers, who are identified as Jotunn maidens. Some scholars have suggested that these nine might be the nine daughters of Aegir and Ran, since Heimdall's legends also claim that his mothers were all sisters and one of his alternate names is Vindler, which can be translated as 'Wind-Sea'. However, a poem normally assumed to refer to Heimdall names nine female Jotnar as the mothers of a god and gives their names. These are different to those of the daughters of Aegir and Ran.

Little is recorded about some of these figures. Angeyja, Atla, Eistla and Ulfrun do not appear elsewhere in the Norse tales, but Gjalp, Greip and Jarnsaxa do have quite prominent roles.

### Gjalp and Greip

Gjalp and Greip were daughters of the Jotunn Geirrod who was an enemy of Thor. He managed to capture Loki while he was in the form of a hawk, and extracted from him a promise to deliver Thor to Geirrod. As usual, Loki agreed to betray his adopted kin

# THOR MET GJALP STANDING ABOVE THE RIVER VIMUR. THOR THREW A ROCK AT HER AND STOPPED THE FLOOD THAT SHE WAS CAUSING.

and convinced Thor to go to Geirrod's abode without his magical gloves or belt, and particularly without his hammer Mjolnir.

On the way, Loki and Thor stopped at the house of a female Jotunn named Grid, who not only informed Thor of the trap he was walking into but gave him the means to reverse the situation. Grid equipped Thor with magical iron gloves, belt and a staff.

Continuing towards Geirrod's house, Thor encountered the Jotunn's daughter, Gjalp, standing with one foot in each of two ravines and urinating into the river Vimur. Thor threw a rock at her and thereby stopped the flood that she was causing. He then went to Geirrod's house where he was shown to a room

ABOVE: On the way to Geirrod's house Thor encountered the giantess Gjalp, who tried to drown him by causing the river Vimur to flood.

containing only a single chair. This is described as the giantess' hat in a kenning, so presumably the giantesses Gjalp and Greip were somehow under it.

When Thor sat down, the giantesses pushed the chair upwards, intending to crush Thor against the ceiling. Instead, he used the magical staff Grid had given him to push against the ceiling, saving himself and breaking the backs of both Jotnar. Thor then confronted Geirrod, who flung a piece of hot iron at him. Again Grid's gifts aided Thor – he caught the iron and threw it back. Although Geirrod hid behind a pillar, the iron went through it, and his head, and into the ground.

## Jarnsaxa

Thor's relations with the giantess Jarnsaxa were rather better. They had two sons together, named Magni and Modi, who survived Ragnarok and inherited Mjolnir. Magni ('Might') had a horse named Gullfaxi who was almost a rival to Sleipnir in speed and agility.

## Other Jotnar

Many Jotnar appear in the Norse tales, often only in passing as someone encountered (or fought, tricked or otherwise defeated) by one of the gods in the course of an adventure. Some of these Jotnar appear to have been important in the grand scheme of things, but were peripheral to the tales of the gods, so receive less attention than they might perhaps deserve.

## Beli

Beli was a Jotunn killed under mysterious circumstances by Freyr. Having given his magic sword to his servant Skirnir, Freyr encountered Beli and killed him using an antler. Apparently Beli was not much of a fighter – in a conversation with King Gylfi, a disguised Odin remarks that Freyr could have slain Beli with his bare hands.

## Egdir (or Eggther)

Egdir is described as the 'herdsman of the giantess' although exactly who this referred to is unclear. She may have been one of the giantesses (possibly Angrboda, mother of Loki's monstrous children) who lived in Jarnvidr ('Iron-wood') somewhere to the east of Midgard and raised broods of giant wolves and other monsters. If so, Egdir presumably looked after the herds of monsters. He is described as playing a harp while waiting for the rooster Fjalar to crow. This rooster had the same name as one of the murderers of Kvasir, but that may just be a coincidence.

The crowing of the rooster signified the beginning of Ragnarok, so in some ways Egdir had the same role as Heimdall, but for the giants rather than the gods. Thus Egdir is considered to be a watchman as well as a herdsman, and a harbinger of Ragnarok.

ABOVE: **Freyr sent Skirnir to persuade Gerd to marry him. His decision to loan Skirnir his sword may have been a mistake – he was without it at Ragnarok and was slain by the fire giant Surt.**

## Gerd

Gerd was a female Jotunn who married the god Freyr. Her mother was Aurboda and her father was Gymir, although the latter is sometimes confused with Aegir. Gymir has at times been considered a sea-giant in the form of a serpent and at others an underworld or earth creature instead.

Gerd was extremely beautiful, which caused Freyr to fall in love with her upon seeing her from a distance. He sent his servant Skirnir to ask Gerd to marry him, which was at first refused. Some versions of the tale include dire threats made by Skirnir, others do not, but in the end Gerd agreed to marry Freyr

and they met at a place called Bari. In order to facilitate his task, Freyr gave his magical sword to Skirnir, perhaps leading to his death in battle at Ragnarok against the fire giant Surt.

## Hraesvelgr

Hraesvelgr was a Jotunn whose name translated as 'Corpse Swallower'. He took the form of an eagle and made the wind blow by flapping his wings. Little is recorded about him; he appears only in a passing reference.

## Hrungnir

Hrungnir, unusually, was a Jotunn who went to Valhol after his death. Even more curiously he did not enter Valhol after a valiant death in battle, but as the result of a lost bet. Offered a wager by Odin that his horse Sleipnir was faster than Hrungnir's mount Gullfaxi, the Jotunn accepted and agreed to forfeit his head as the price for losing.

Arriving in Valhol, which was populated by warriors who endlessly drank and fought, Hrungnir became so drunk and argumentative that no one could stand him and the gods had to take action. Thor was sent to fight Hrungnir, who was armed with a whetstone. This he hurled at Thor, who smashed it with Mjolnir. Fragments of the stone landed in Midgard, and henceforth flint could be found in that land.

One piece of the whetstone lodged in Thor's head, although by this point he had struck Hrungnir dead. He fell and was pinned under the foot of the fallen Jotunn until rescued by the giantess Jarnsaxa, who brought their infant child Magni to help. Magni was so strong even as a child that he was able to free his father, even though all of the Aesir combined could not lift

Hrungnir's foot. Hrungnir was assisted in this fight by Mokkurkalfi, a giant constructed out of clay. Although truly enormous, Mokkurkalfi was very slow and was terrified of Thor. He was defeated by Thor's servant Thjalfi.

An attempt was made to remove the stone fragment from Thor's head with the assistance of the sorceress Groa. This was working well until Thor told her that he had recently assisted her husband Aurvandil and that he was on his way home. Excited to be reunited with her husband, Groa forgot her magical chants and the stone remained stuck.

## Hrym

Hrym was a Jotun who captained the ship *Naglfar*. This vessel carried the legions of the dead from Helheim to the battle of Ragnarok. Some sources cite Loki as the captain of this ship, but even so Hrym is still noted as arriving for the battle aboard it.

## Hyrokkin

When Baldr died, he was placed in a funeral ship surrounded by grave-goods and accompanied by his wife Nanna, who had died of grief. The boat was called *Hringhorni*, and it was so large and heavily loaded that none of the gods could launch it. They asked for help, and from Jotunheim came the giantess Hyrokkin who was renowned for her incredible strength.

Hyrokkin rode a giant wolf, using vipers as reins, and the beast was so savage that Odin's attending guards had to render it unconscious before they could control it. Hyrokkin then launched the funeral boat, using just one hand to do what all the gods combined had failed to accomplish. The violence of the launch caused sparks and flames, which naturally angered Thor. It is possible to surmise that in fact Thor, renowned for his strength, was annoyed at being upstaged by a giantess. In either case he prepared to slay Hyrokkin, but was dissuaded by the other Aesir.

ABOVE: The Tullstorp runestone depicts the ship *Naglfar* bringing the dead to the plain of Virior to fight the last battle of Ragnarok. The wolf Fenrir is also shown, though he did not travel aboard the nail-ship.

OPPOSITE: The Jotunn Hrungnir hurled a whetstone at Thor's head, where it became embedded. An attempt to remove the stone by the sorceress Groa was derailed when she became distracted by news about her husband.

## Modgud

Modgud, whose name translates as 'Furious Battler' was a Jotunn tasked with guarding the entrance to the domain of Hel. This was a bridge over the river Gjoll ('Noisy'), which was one of the 11 great rivers originating from the Well of Hvergelmir. The water was very cold, as it came straight from Niflheim's heart, and the only way to cross was the bridge Gjallarbru. Modgud would permit the newly dead to cross the bridge into Helheim, but would stop them coming out again. She was encountered by Hermod when he went to ask Hel if she would release Baldr.

## Skrymir (Utgarda-Loki)

Skrymir was the king of the Jotnar and the lord of Jotunheim. He was sometimes also known as Utgarda-Loki, which can cause confusion – in fact he was nothing to do with the trickster-god Loki, although he was also a master of illusion.

Utgarda-Loki used his magic and illusions to confuse Thor and his companions, stealing their food and humiliating Thor before he even arrived at Skrymir's castle. Thor and his companions took shelter in a building during their journey, finding it strangely dark inside. They were awoken during the night by strange noises and found the building was shaking. The companions hid in a side room where Thor stood guard over them.

After a very unpleasant and frightening night, the travellers went outside and found a sleeping giant, whose snores were shaking the land. The giant awoke and said his name was Skrymir, then picked up a glove he had taken off to sleep. This was the 'building' that Thor and his friends had taken shelter in; they had retreated into the thumb when Skrymir's snores frightened them. Skrymir suggested that they all go to his castle together, and offered to carry their packs. Even without the weight of their packs, the travellers found Skrymir difficult to keep up with. When he stopped for the night and went to sleep, Thor and the others caught up and tried to get food from his pack. He had fastened the straps so tightly that Thor could not get at the food, which angered him to the point where he smashed the giant in the head with Mjolnir.

The blow merely woke Skrymir, who asked if a leaf had fallen on him. He went back to sleep and began snoring again, keeping the companions awake. Thor struck him again, but with no apparent effect other than to wake the giant. After Skrymir went to sleep again, Thor struck him as hard as he could, burying Mjolnir in the giant's brain. To Thor's dismay, Skrymir awoke and asked if bird droppings had fallen on him.

Skrymir then parted company from the travellers, pausing only to insult Thor. He told the god not to brag in the castle of Utgarda-Loki as the giants would not tolerate it from someone

ABOVE: The giant Skrymir amused himself at Thor's expense, playing tricks and using illusions to humiliate the proud god. Thor responded with repeated attempts to murder Skrymir in his sleep, none of which were successful as a result of Skrymir's magic.

as puny as Thor. The companions then walked for another day before they reached the castle of Utgarda-Loki, which was so huge that they could barely see the top of it.

Inside the castle, the gods were received by Utgarda-Loki, King of the Giants, and challenged to a series of contests that they could not possibly win. When Thor was asked to show his strength by picking up a cat, it was in fact the world-serpent Jormungand disguised by magic. His wrestling match turned out to be against old age, and a challenge to drink the contents of a horn was also rigged – it was magically connected to the sea.

BELOW: The Jotunn Skrymir was a giant in the usual sense of the word. His castle was so huge that Thor and his companions could barely see the highest parts of it.

Meanwhile Thjalfi, Thor's servant, was challenged to a race, only to find that his opponent was swifter than anything else in creation. This was a being named 'Hugi', which translates as 'thought'. Loki was challenged to an eating contest, but his opponent turned out to be fire itself, which consumes everything.

Having had his fun (or, perhaps, taught the gods a little humility), Utgarda-Loki sent them on their way. He explained that he was Skrymir and that he had used his magic to deceive Thor in the wilderness. The pack had been wired shut; a hill had stood between Skrymir's head and Mjolnir, and was now dented by three deep valleys. He also explained that the contests had been rigged and that the gods' performance had greatly exceeded his expectations. He added that if he had known how mighty Thor actually was he would never have allowed him inside the castle. None of this did anything to mollify Thor, but as the angry god raised his hammer to attack Skrymir and his castle, it vanished.

'BRING THE HAMMER SO THAT WE MAY CONSECRATE THE BRIDE.' – POETIC EDDA

## Suttung

Suttung was the son of Gilling and his wife, both of whom were murdered by the Dwarfs Fjalar and Galar just for the fun of it. In his quest for vengeance Suttung obtained the Mead of Poetry from the Dwarfs, and gave it to his daughter Gunnlod to look after. Suttung's brother, Baugi, was then tricked into assisting Odin in getting into Suttung's home, where he seduced Gunnlod and stole the mead.

BELOW: Odin deceived and seduced Gunnlod in order to get access to the Mead of Poetry, then stole it and left her to face the wrath of her father, Suttung. He escaped in the form of an eagle.

## Thokk

When Baldr was slain, Hel agreed to release him if everyone in the cosmos would weep for him. Messengers were sent out asking all the people of the worlds to do so, and everyone did except for a giantess named Thokk. Thokk was encountered in a cave as the messengers went home thinking they had achieved their aim. Her refusal meant that Baldr would have to remain with Hel. Thokk was, of course, Loki in disguise, completing his betrayal of his blood brother Odin by ensuring that his son Baldr stayed dead.

## Thrym

Thrym was the King of the Jotnar and lord of Jotunheim. Wanting the goddess Freyja for his wife, he contrived to steal Thor's hammer Mjolnir and demanded the goddess in return. Thrym was tricked into thinking that the gods had agreed, and that the heavily disguised Thor who arrived at his hall was in fact Freyja. Seizing his hammer, Thor then slew Thrym and everyone else in the hall.

## Vafprudnir

Vafprudnir, whose name translates as 'mighty weaver' in reference to the riddles he posed, was a very powerful and wise Jotunn who knew much about the past and the future. Odin visited his hall to engage in a riddling contest to see who was wiser; the overconfident Vafprudnir wagered his head and lost it. This, more than Odin's victory in the contest, suggests that Vafprudnir was less wise than he thought.

Odin more or less cheated in the contest by asking a question that only he could know the answer to – what did Odin whisper in dead Baldr's ear at his funeral? Engaging in a lethal contest against someone as slippery as Odin might well be a pointless undertaking.

OPPOSITE: The Jotunn Thrym tried to coerce Freyja into marrying him, but a heavily disguised Thor went in her place. As soon as he had Mjolnir back in his hands, Thor tore off the bridal veil and went on a rampage in Thrym's hall.

4

# OTHER CREATURES

Norse mythology tells of a variety of magical creatures, the nature of which is not as clear-cut as modern thinking might suggest. Indeed, it is possible that the beings described in any given tale are unique to it and not in any way related to those with similar names or characteristics in others.

Attempts to neatly codify the powers and abilities of each 'race' of mythical creatures inevitably founder upon the rocks of vagueness and distortion. Since the original tales cannot at times agree on whether a given individual is a god, Jotunn or mortal, it is rather unlikely that the supernatural and magical beings encountered by the gods are treated any more consistently.

## The Disir and Fylgja

The Norse tales contain references to spirits called Disir, whose nature is not clear. It is possible that the Disir are ancestral spirits or perhaps Elves, or it may be that the term is a catch-all for supernatural beings; a hypothesis borne out by references to Valkyries as 'Odin's Disir'. However, the term 'Disir' seems to apply mainly to female spirits, or beings who are generally beneficial. This does not mean that they are not warlike – some are very much so – but whether helping in battle or healing the sick, they seem to be seeking a positive outcome for the subject of their actions.

Very little is recorded about these spirits, but it is known that during the winter it was customary (in some areas at least) to hold a festival that included a sacrifice to the Disir. Given the nature of winter festivals in general, this was likely a religious or spiritual occasion intended to ward off the worst of the winter and ensure a good start to the new year, and was probably accompanied by a feast of some sort. However, very little concrete information is available.

## The Norns

The Norns were magical creatures connected with fate and destiny. There were in fact many norns (with no capitalization),

in the sense that the word referred to a practitioner of magic. In theory, any human seer or sorceress, and many magical creatures including the gods Odin and Frigg, could be described as norns. Norse mythology refers to three Norns (with capitalization) as being of primary importance, and it is these three that are referred to when using the capitalized Norns.

The three Norns were named Urd, Verdandi and Skuld, translating to 'what was once', 'what (imminently) comes to be' and 'what shall be in the future'. It is easy to translate this to 'past, present and future' but this is overly simplistic. Unlike the Fates in Greek mythology, the Norns did not dictate an exact fate for any given person. Instead they described potentialities and possibilities in an endless cycle.

Urd ('what was once') represented all that had gone before, which in turn dictated the options available at the present time. A decision made in the past might close off some options that otherwise could have been available, so the past shaped not merely the conditions of the present, but also the options available in it.

Verdandi ('what is coming to be') represented the present situation and the available options, and also

## SPIRITUAL COMPANIONS

Some individuals had companion spirits, which were in certain cases almost separate entities (such as Odin's ravens) and in most others tied closely to the person they followed. Odin's ravens and wolves – and, according to some sources, the Valkyries – were essentially parts of his being made corporeal and given a semi-independent existence. Less powerful beings instead had a fylgjur, which translates as 'follower'.

The form taken by a fylgjur reflected the personality of the individual they were associated with. The companion spirits of those who could do magic often took the form of cats and birds to those that could see them, creating parallels to the familiars used by sorcerers and witches in European folklore. However, most people would not be able to see their fylgjur, which was a good thing – when one appeared to its associated human, it was often an indication of imminent death.

the instant in which decisions were made. These decisions would open up some future options and close off others, so a decision made in the present would affect the conditions of any given future instant, and also the options available at that time. Thus Skuld ('what shall be in the future') depended very much on what had gone before, further modified by decisions made in the present.

This was a constant cycle. Decisions made in the present would soon become part of the past, further dictating the course of the future by limiting the options of the new present. This cycle was represented by the way the Norns took water from the Well of Urd and used it to nourish Yggdrasil, from whose branches it fell back into the well.

The great tree can also be taken as a metaphor for the cyclical nature of past, present and future. The roots of the tree are the past, they are already there and they limit how big the tree can grow, as well as

ABOVE: **An illustration inspired by Wagner's 'Ring Cycle' of operas shows the Norns weaving the rope of destiny beside Yggdrasil. Their role seems largely to be observers and chroniclers – they did not dictate the fate of people.**

## USING MAGIC TO CHANGE THE FUTURE

Magic could affect the course of events and the probabilities of any given outcome, and for that reason practitioners of magic can also be considered to be norns. Something as simple as a spell to improve eloquence could greatly affect the course of the future by enabling a god or hero to persuade others to take a given course of action. A spell to ward off poison in a drink could ensure that a person's fate did not end then and there, making possible a range of futures that would otherwise not have existed. Thus Norse magic can be seen in the context of altering fate and creating new possibilities, but it could not change what had already happened, and thus was limited in its ability to alter the universe in sudden, large-scale ways.

its nature. Only an ash tree can grow from an ash tree root, and since Yggdrasil's roots are those of an ash tree, a future in which Yggdrasil is a beech is not possible.

The trunk is the present, the point from which branches sprout. It is possible to decide which branch to proceed along, but that choice once made cannot be changed. It is now part of the past and shapes the possible futures. Once on a branch, it is only possible to encounter what is there. Perhaps it is the squirrel Ratatosk, racing up and down the tree passing poisonous messages between the enemy eagle and dragon. If so, more decisions await – such as what to do about whatever Ratatosk has to say.

Going along a different branch might mean not meeting Ratatosk and thus not having those options, but might instead lead to an encounter with Heidrun, the goat that stands atop Odin's hall. This would give a different set of options, possibly leading to a quite different future. Thus the choices made in (and the conditions of) the past dictate the options of the present, and those in turn shape the possible form of the future. The range of possibilities is defined by fate, but the actual course of events is dictated by the choices made along the way.

## The Valkyries and Other Mystical Warriors

The Valkyries (or Valkyrja) were choosers of the slain. Their task was to decide which warriors would be taken to Folkvangr or Valhol to prepare for the great battle of Ragnarok. The rest were the concern of Hel, but Odin wanted the best of the best to fight on his side in the final battle.

BELOW: The Valkyries could assist human warriors in battle, either with magic or by joining the fight in person. They seem to have had a certain amount of choice about which side to join, and were at times willing to disobey orders.

# BRYNHILD, VALKYRIE SHIELDMAIDEN

Most famous of the Valkyries is Brynhild, who had a falling-out with Odin after disobeying him. Two rival kings, Agnar and Hjalmgunnar, were engaged in battle and Odin wanted Hjalmgunnar to win. However, Brynhild arranged matters so that Agnar would be victorious. For this she was punished to live as a mortal. This tale is referred to in several Norse sagas and Germanic epic poems, and from the latter was derived Wagner's 'Ring Cycle' of operas of 1876.

ABOVE: 'Brynhild stands for a long time, dazed and alarmed', by Arthur Rackham (1910).

The Valkyries are usually depicted in modern times as beautiful warrior-women, and there is evidence from the Norse tales that they could be attractive. Many Valkyries are noted as being the daughters of royalty. Some became lovers of human warriors, heroes and kings, and bore them children. However, the original form of the Valkyries, at least some of the time, was rather less pleasant. Associated with death and the aftermath of battle, Valkyries are often depicted as accompanied by crows and other carrion-eating creatures, but in fact this may have been the form in which they came to the battlefield.

There is some evidence that the original 'real' Valkyries were hags who tended sacred groves where human sacrifice took place. Human sacrifice was not prevalent, but probably occurred at times of great crisis. According to some sources, sacrifices were made to Odin by hanging men from trees, in the manner of Odin's self-impalement, and that captured warriors could be sacrificed to Odin using a spear. If so, then the original Valkyrie may have been elderly priestesses who decided who was worthy of being sacrificed, or how important an individual was required to ensure an end to the present crisis. Records indicate that sacrifices were mainly captives and outlaws, but on one occasion a king was sacrificed to end a desperate famine.

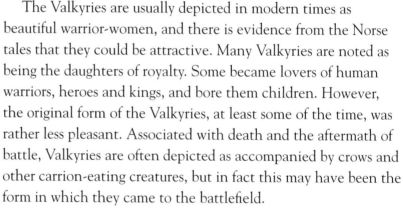

The mythical Valkyries did not merely choose who among the slain was worthy of Folkvangr or Valhol, they also had a hand in choosing who would be slain. Valkyries could use magic to assist or hamper whoever they thought deserved it, and could alter the course of a battle or the fate of an individual warrior by this means. When not out in the world as choosers or lovers of mortal warriors, the Valkyries also brought mead to the dead warriors of Valhol.

ABOVE: The afterlife of the Einherjar was filled with endless violence. To recuperate they spent the nights in comradely feasting, drinking mead served by Valkyries and presumably boasting of their deeds in the day's battles.

## Einherjar

The Einherjar were warriors who had been chosen after death for entry to Valhol. There, they fought constantly to practice for the coming battle, and were healed of their wounds at the end of each day. Even severed heads and limbs were renewed, and the Einherjar then spent the night in feasting. The number of Einherjar is not known, although Odin responded to speculation that there are indeed a large number of warriors in Valhol, but the food never ran out and the doorways were never crowded. He added that as many as there are, the Einherjar would seem too few 'when the wolf comes', a reference to the arrival of Fenrir at the battle of Ragnarok.

OPPOSITE This sixth-century Swedish silver-gilt pendant shows a female spirit of some power. The subject is probably a Valkyrie, but could be one of the Disir. It may have been carried in the hope of invoking the assistance of the spirit.

# Berserkers

Berserkers, or berserks, appear in tales of Norse gods and heroes, and also in history. The 'real' berserks are a source of much confusion. Most people are familiar with the idea that they were warriors who disregarded their own safety and essentially went kill-crazy in battle for a variety of reasons. It has been suggested that the berserks were individuals suffering from a dissociative

ABOVE: **Despite being mad as dogs, Berserkers were highly skilled warriors who exploited their invulnerability to fire and iron to demolish their enemies.**

personality disorder similar to the phenomenon of 'running amok' in the Malay language, and that this disorder, or symptoms similar to it, was induced by religious fervour and/or drugs of some kind.

It has also been suggested that berserkers were nothing more than a tribe who were known to be very good at fighting, or a bodyguard force picked by warrior kings for their prowess in battle. The confidence, aggression and perhaps bravado of these individuals might come across as reckless disregard for survival or even lunacy. Various linguistic interpretations of 'berserk' have been put forward, including men who wore bearskin cloaks as a symbol of their status as great warriors, or men who fought 'bare chested'. This may not have actually meant discarding clothes and armour before a battle; a man who fought without a shield might also be considered bare-chested.

The 'Berserkr' of myth are of course associated with Odin. They are inspired by his reckless fury or ecstasy, and are described as fighting without armour while being as mad as dogs. Despite throwing away their protection, these warriors were apparently invulnerable to both fire and iron. The Berserkr were said to change form when they 'went berserk', the act of which was termed 'berserkergang'. This does not necessarily translate to turning into animals; it more probably refers to the change of state from a fairly rational professional warrior into a divinely-inspired slaughter-machine.

A Berserkr was also alleged to be able to use magic. Traditional Norse folklore included various charms and practices to prevent a Berserkr from rendering blunt a warrior's weapon. This was one of their powers, and may have contributed to the impression that iron could not harm them – a blow with even a blunt sword would be enough to stop many warriors in their tracks, but one who was in a mental state where he disregarded pain and fear would not be much affected by anything that did not immediately put him down.

## Land Spirits

The Landvaettir (which translates as 'land wights') are spirits or magical beings tied to and associated with a particular place. The origin of these land spirits is unclear, but they definitely did not need the presence of mortals to come into being. When Iceland was first discovered, it was completely uninhabited except for a handful of extremely hardy Irish monks who departed when the Norsemen arrived. Despite the fact that Iceland had only ever been inhabited by Christians, there were powerful Norse land spirits already there.

The first real colonization attempt occurred in 870 AD, led by foster-brothers Hjorleifur Hrooarson and Ingolfur Arnarson. Ingolfur decided to let the gods and the spirits of the land guide him to a suitable place to live, and had his men throw the pillars that normally flanked his high-seat overboard. These were a symbol of his power and leadership, so surrendering them to the gods and spirits was clearly the action of a devout man.

The pillars were washed out of sight by the tide, and it took three years to find them. All of that time, Ingolfur's colonists and livestock

BELOW: Ingolfur Arnarson was suitably respectful towards the land-spirits of Iceland, and was thus the founder of a thriving settlement. This statue in Reykjavik commemorates him.

had to wait, taking temporary shelter, despite the fact that there was good land for a settlement clearly available. In the end, the pillars were found on a rocky headland that seemed to be less than attractive as a place to live. Nevertheless, Ingolfur settled there and established a colony that grew to be modern-day Reykjavík, capital of Iceland.

## EGIL SKALLAGRIMSSON TURNED THE LAND SPIRITS AGAINST HIS ENEMIES.

Ingolfur's foster-brother Hjorleifur, on the other hand, fared less well. He simply found a good spot and landed there. Prospects initially seemed good as the new arrivals built a settlement and began farming the land. However, the slaves they had brought with them to assist in setting up the colony revolted and killed everyone in the settlement.

The Landvaettir were mostly minor local spirits, but Iceland was protected by four great spirits who took the forms of a great eagle, a giant, a dragon and a bull, and led other land spirits to oppose invaders. These four great spirits each guarded one quarter of Iceland, and today appear on the nation's coins.

The land spirits were necessary to the fertility and general wellbeing of the area they were associated with. Often tied to a specific feature such as a boulder, they could be good neighbours to those who respected them, but might harass and victimize offenders. This was exploited by the Icelandic hero Egil Skallagrimsson, who set up magical poles to confuse and upset the land spirits so that they would turn against his enemies.

ABOVE: **Modern Icelandic coins depict the four great land spirits who are the guardians of Iceland. They are a bull, an eagle, a giant and a dragon, and can rouse other spirits to aid them.**

The Landvaettir could also be frightened off or agitated by other means. One of the very few pieces of evidence for the existence of 'dragon ships' is a prohibition on ships with a prow shaped like a dragon's head from approaching the land or entering harbour in case it alarmed the land spirts. This appears in the *Landnamabok*, or *Book of Settlement*, a history of the early years in Iceland that was probably written in the thirteenth century.

The land spirits were revered in Iceland long after Christianity supplanted the old Norse religion. Indeed, today there are still particular rocks that are carefully left alone. The Landvaettir are not worshipped so much as afforded the polite respect owed

to a good neighbour. They are, apparently, willing to return the courtesy and to accommodate respectful humans. During the construction of the Naval Air Station at Keflavik in southwest Iceland in the 1940s, one of the construction team was asked in a dream to grant time for the local Landvaettir to move out of a boulder that was scheduled for removal. This was granted, and the boulder was not removed until a second dream indicated that the land spirits had found a new home.

ABOVE: According to legend, the basalt stacks at Reynisdrangar were formerly trolls named Skessudranggur, Laddrangur and Langhamar, who were caught in the sunlight and turned to stone.

## Elves and Dwarfs

In modern times, there are clear distinctions between what we think of as 'Dwarfs' and 'Elves'. This is mainly the result of fantasy stories that use a similar basic definition of these creatures. The details may vary, but as a rule we have come to think of Elves as somewhat magical people who are in tune with nature and probably live in a forest, and Dwarfs as hardy folk who live under mountains and produce magical or technological wonders. These tropes are derived from Norse mythology, but the original versions of the Elf and Dwarf folk were far more complex.

In fact, it is not clear whether references to 'Light Elves', 'Dark Elves' and 'Dwarfs' relate to different groups at all. The characteristics of these various groups are at times interchanged in the original tales, along with the names of their homelands. In particular, the Dark Elves and the Dwarfs of Norse legend might well be the same people. Alternatively, references to a creature as an Elf or Dwarf might not refer to a race or species at all.

Just as the Jotunn vary enormously in size, physical appearance and capabilities, and might better be described as a mystical or social grouping than a race or species, so it may be that certain beings of power are described as Dwarfs or Elves, not because they belong to a certain species, but because they have the powers, attitudes and capabilities that make them fit that group's general characteristics. That said, it is possible to identify three main groups: Light Elves, Dark Elves and Dwarfs. Some references are contradictory, but a general picture can be discerned of each group.

According to some sources, Elves have the ability to both cause and cure sickness in humans, and will help people in return for sacrifices. Even after the old Norse gods were supplanted by Christianity, some groups continued to sacrifice to and worship Elves. This was outlawed by Christian authorities, but continued anyway, similar to the respect for land spirits that continues to this day. It may be that there is no real distinction between land spirits and Elves.

BELOW: **The Dwarfs seem to have interacted quite often with the gods, and were sufficiently respectful of their power that they furnished lavish gifts when asked to do so. They were the source of all the magical treasures owned by the gods.**

Other interactions are also possible, including the creation of half-Elf children and the possibility of a human becoming an Elf or similar spirit after death. However, this may be a confusion deriving from the worship of ancestors that took place in some areas. It is not at all clear where the line between venerated ancestors, Landvaettir and Elves lay – or even if one existed.

## The Ljosalfar (Light Elves)

The Ljosalfar lived in Alfheim, which lay close to Asgard, and were extremely beautiful. For reasons that are not clear, Freyr was the ruler of Alfheim, although he was not explicitly stated to be the leader of the Light Elves. The Ljosalfar seem to have been friendly to the gods, particularly the Vanir, but are not recorded as being very active in any of the tales. They seem to have been content to dwell in Alfheim and let everything else take its course.

> THE ELVES ARE LUMINOUS BEINGS, 'MORE BEAUTIFUL THAN THE SUN.'
> – *PROSE EDDA*

It is possible that the Ljosalfar represented an older set of gods who were displaced by the Asgardian deities, perhaps as a result of migrant people with their own gods moving into Scandinavia and becoming dominant. The same has been said about the Vanir, and given the close relationship and similarities between the Ljosalfar and the Vanir it is not impossible that they were two versions of the same mythic group; old gods relegated to a lesser role by upstart newcomers. It is equally possible that there were two such events – the old gods represented by the Ljosalfar were supplanted by the Vanir, who were then relegated to second place as society changed and more martial gods became prevalent.

## The Dokkalfar/Svartalfar (Dark Elves/Black Elves)

The Dokkalfar (Dark Elves) were probably the same beings occasionally referred to as Svartalfar (Black Elves), although this term may instead refer to Dwarfs. There are indications that the Dokkalfar were not dark in colour as such, but merely dimmer and less luminous than the Ljosalfar. They were more mischievous and malicious than their lighter cousins, and have been blamed for causing nightmares by sitting on the chest of a

ABOVE: Not all interactions between the gods and the dwarfs were amicable. This 1878 painting shows dwarfs fleeing in terror from one of Thor's spectacular rages. Thor murdered the dwarf Lit by kicking him into Baldr's funeral pyre.

sleeping human and putting grim thoughts into their mind. The Dark Elves are sometimes stated to live in Svartalfheim, although some sources claim that this was the home of the Dwarfs. It is quite possible that both lived there, or that the dwellers of Svartalfheim included some beings that could be identified as Dark Elves and some better categorized as Dwarfs.

## The Duergar (Dwarfs)

Dwarfs feature more prominently in the Norse tales than either group of Elves. They were not inimical to the gods, although some met an unfortunate fate at their hands. When the Dwarf Lit attended Baldr's funeral, he got in Thor's way, so the angry god kicked him into the funeral pyre. Lit does not seem to have done much to deserve this fate.

Some, like Fjalar and Galar, were both greedy and psychotic. Their murder of Kvasir to obtain his wisdom is perhaps understandable: it was a terrible act born out of rampant greed. However, they then killed the giant Gilling for no good reason, and also his wife, because the sounds of her grief bothered them. Fjalar and Galar were an exception, however. Most Dwarfs seem to have had their own agenda and were not malicious towards those who did not interfere with it.

The Dwarfs lived underground in a realm stated as being called either Svartalfheim or Nidavellir. It is tempting to believe that the Light Elves lived in Alfheim, the Dark Elves in Svartalfheim and the Dwarfs in Nidavellir, but this is probably too simplistic. Distinctions between the groups are not sufficiently clear-cut to make such a neat and tidy definition. However, it is repeatedly stated that the Dwarfs were master craftsmen who made great magical treasures and lived underground in mines and caverns. It is in their capacity as makers that they are most commonly encountered by the gods.

## The Four First Dwarfs

Not all of the Dwarfs lived underground. Soon after the slaying of Ymir, maggots began to crawl out of his flesh. These were the first of the Dwarfs, and the very first four to emerge were given tasks by the gods. These four, named Nordri, Sudri, Austri and Vestri, were ordered to hold up the skull of Ymir, from which had been fashioned the sky, and gave their names to the cardinal points of the compass.

## The Great Craftsmen

After Loki cut off Sif's hair and was threatened with punishment by Thor, he offered to replace it. Naturally, he turned to the great craftsmen of the Dwarfs to produce something that would please Sif and placate her husband. The Dwarf craftsman Ivadi produced the necessary item; a replacement for Sif's hair made of real gold, which would grow naturally once she wore it. He also provided the magical ship *Skidbladnir* to be given to Freyr and the spear Gungnir for Odin.

BELOW: Dwarfs were particularly adept at working with silver and gold. Although they are often depicted as avaricious in modern fantasy, those in the original myths were not excessively concerned with hoarding treasure.

Loki then engineered a contest in which the Dwarf smiths Brokk and Eitri (sometimes referred to as Sindri) tried to make even better gifts for the gods. They made a golden boar named Gullin-Borsti for Freyr, the magical arm-ring Draupnir for Odin and the hammer Mjolnir for Thor. Although Loki's interference caused the hammer to be slightly defective, these were still gifts that pleased the gods.

ABOVE: **The dwarf smiths Brokk and Eitri tried to outdo their peers by making even better gifts for the gods. Their greatest creation, despite Loki's interference, was the hammer Mjolnir, which was given to Thor.**

The master smith Alviss wanted to marry Thor's daughter Thrud. Thor did not like this idea at all, so demanded that Alviss prove his great wisdom. Although not normally a great thinker, Thor managed to keep Alviss talking until daybreak, when the sun's rays turned Alviss to stone. This trait is often associated with trolls, a term sometimes used interchangeably with 'giant' in later Scandinavian mythology.

Nabbi and Dain were the makers of the magical boar Hildisvini, which was ridden by Freyja. Loki claimed that the boar was actually Freyr's human lover Ottar in disguise, but there may or may not have been any substance to this claim. The two Dwarfs also made a cursed sword named Dainsleif. It was a powerful weapon that never failed to kill or maim its target, but once unsheathed it could not be returned to its scabbard without slaying a man.

Alfrigg, Berling, Dvalin and Grerr were four other great craftsmen. They made a magical necklace of great beauty called Brisingamen, and Freyr wanted it. The four refused all monetary offers, but agreed to give Freya the necklace if she spent the night with each of them.

Andvari was yet another great craftsman who made an arm-ring with the same properties as Draupnir. Named Andvarinaut, it would drop eight copies of itself every ninth night. Andvari lived under a waterfall and could turn himself into a fish. Needing gold to pay a 'weregild' ('man-price'), Loki borrowed

a net from Ran, a goddess associated with the sea, and caught Andvari in fish form. Loki took the arm-ring along with the rest of the Dwarf's gold, but Andvari laid a curse on it that brought disaster upon all future owners. These included the Dwarf King Hreidmar.

Hreidmar had two daughters, Lofnheid and Lyngheid, and three sons named Fafnir, Otr and Regin. Otr had the ability to turn himself into an otter, and while in this form he was encountered by Thor and Loki on their travels. Loki killed the otter with a hurled stone (the tale seems to imply that this was a genuine mistake and not some convoluted prank on Loki's part), and the two showed off the fine pelt that night at the home of Hreidmar, where they were staying.

Hreidmar naturally was angered and took the gods hostage, sending Loki away to gather a ransom sufficient to fill the otter's pelt with gold. Among the items Loki brought was the ring Andvarinaut, which was now cursed. The gods went on their way and soon the curse manifested itself. Fafnir went insane with greed and slew his father to get the ring.

ABOVE: Having taken all of the Dwarf Andvari's gold, except the ring Andvarinaut, Loki decided he wanted that, too. Andvari cursed the ring to bring misfortune upon all who owned it. The family of King Hreidmar was subsequently destroyed.

# Fafnir and Other Dragons

After murdering his father and fleeing into the wilderness, Fafnir's insanity and greed caused him to turn into a dragon. Not only did he viciously protect his hoard of gold, but he poisoned the land with his breath. His brother Regin sent his foster-son Sigurd to slay the beast and gain vengeance. He was apparently not a Dwarf of great courage, for after advising Regin to dig a trench to hide in and ambush Fafnir as he went to drink, Regin fled.

Odin, who perhaps saw greatness in Sigurd, lent a hand in the guise of a passing wise man. He suggested that Sigurd dig several trenches to allow the dragon's blood to drain away, and thus avoid drowning in it. Then Odin, too, left Sigurd to his task. Sigurd lay in the trench and when Fafnir crawled over him he stabbed the dragon through the shoulder with his sword Gram.

The two conversed as Fafnir lay dying, and in response to the dragon's questions about his family, Sigurd revealed that his foster-father was Regin. Fafnir warned Sigurd that Regin would cause his death as well, and that his gold was cursed. Sigurd declared he was not afraid since all men die, and being rich until that day was a good ambition.

Sigurd took the gold back to his foster-father, along with Fafnir's heart which Regin wanted to eat. He planned to murder Sigurd and keep the treasure from the dragon's hoard for himself, but Sigurd learned of this from listening to the birds. He could understand them as a result of ingesting some of Fafnir's blood, and was warned in time to kill Regin, again using his magical sword Gram.

The other dragon that features prominently in the Norse myths is Nidhogg, who lay trapped beneath a root of Yggdrasil in Niflheim and passed the time by alternately gnawing at it and sucking the blood out of corpses. Nidhogg finally got free in time for Ragnarok. He is not explicitly stated as joining the battle, although he did eat many of the corpses from it.

BELOW: **Fafnir is here depicted as a serpent rather than the winged dragon popular in modern fantasy.**

OPPOSITE: **Learning that his foster-father Regin intended to murder him, Sigurd was forced to kill him, too.**

ABOVE: There are many versions of the slaying of Fafnir. In this one, Dwarfs (possibly relatives of King Hreidmar) approach the corpse to ensure the great beast is truly dead. This version of Fafnir is serpentine with no wings.

There are many serpents in Norse mythology, of whom the greatest is Jormungand. This was a giant venomous serpent rather than a winged dragon in the sense that the term is now applied, but once again the dragon of modern fantasy and pseudo-mythology is not the only form that this beast can take. Many descriptions of dragons in mythology mention only that they are great serpents, not necessarily winged and fire breathing.

## Wolves and Other Creatures

Several wolves feature in the Norse mythos. Some are evil, others merely savage and dangerous. Among the former are Skoll and Hati Hroovitnisson, whose names can loosely be translated as 'treachery' and 'hatred'. They pursued the magical horses Skinfaxi and Hrimfaxi, who drew the chariots of the sun and moon respectively. As Ragnarok approached, they would finally catch up and swallow both the sun and the moon. This contradicts other myths where it is Fenrir or some other wolf that ate the sun, but it may be that all these wolves are personifications of the same inimical force, or aspects of Fenrir.

Geri and Freki are Odin's wolves. Both names translate as 'ravenous', but they were not evil, just hungry. Since Odin needed nothing but wine and mead to sustain him, the wolves received everything else served to their master. The names Geri and Freki are often used by skalds as kennings for 'wolf'.

Odin also had two ravens, Hugin and Munin, whose names translate as 'thought' and 'desire' (or perhaps 'memory'). These names are also used kennings, sometimes for ravens and sometimes for associated subjects such as carrion or death. The ravens were given the power of speech by Odin and flew out every day to bring their master news. They are also associated with death, in keeping with Odin's role as a 'psychopomp' (spirit guide) and god of at least some of the dead.

ABOVE: Odin's ravens Hugin and Munin were separate beings, but also an extension of Odin himself. Their role was more that of spies or scouts than carrion birds; both flew out each day to bring their master news from the wider world.

## Humans

Humans have little part to play in the stories of the gods and Jotunn, although they are present in various forms. Warriors populate Valhol and Folkvang after their death, and others go to the realm of Hel. Angry corpses form part of the army led by Loki at Ragnarok. These are peripheral roles, however. Few humans feature directly or are named, although there are tales of human heroes in the Eddas and other sources.

## Ask and Embla

Ask and Embla were the first humans, created by the gods from trees they encountered soon after slaying Ymir. The gods Odin, Vili and Ve gave humans the gifts of inspiration, intellect and warmth of life as well as naming them and creating a place for them to dwell. This was Midgard, protected from the Jotunn by a fence made from Ymir's eyebrows.

## Lif and Lifthrasir

Lif and Lifthrasir were the last two humans, or perhaps the first of the new race of humans. They are variously described as surviving Ragnarok by hiding in Hoddmir's forest, or by being sheltered by Yggdrasil – both could be alternate phrases for the same thing. Once the world was renewed, Lif and Lifthrasir were able to repopulate it with humans.

## Thjalfi and Roskva

On the way to the castle of Skrymir, Thor and his companions stopped at the house of a human family and Thor fed everyone by killing his magical goats Tanngrisnir and Tanngnjostr. The goats could be returned to life so long as their bones were left in the skins overnight, but when the hungry human Thjalfi cracked a bone to get at the marrow, he ensured that one of the goats would be lame.

THOR TOOK THJALFI AND HIS SISTER ROSKVA AS SERVANTS AS PUNISHMENT FOR CRACKING THE GOAT'S BONE.

Thor took Thjalfi and his sister Roskva as servants as punishment for this offence. Thjalfi seems to have been a good companion to Thor, fighting alongside him and even slaying the gigantic clay monster Mokkurkalfi.

Thjalfi fared less well against the women of Hlesey, where a band of women attacked Thor's ship and drove his servant off. In one tale, Thor recounted how he fought these attackers, and was reminded that fighting women is shameful. He countered by pointing out that they were 'she-wolves' and scarcely women at all, suggesting that if women choose to disregard the usual prohibition on cutting their hair short, wearing men's clothes and arming themselves then they could not expect to receive the usual protection from harm.

## Sol and Mani

Sol and Mani were the children of a man named Mundilfari. They were so beautiful that he named them after the sun and moon. His arrogance angered the gods, who took them and placed them in the sky. Sol rode a chariot pulled by two horses named Arvakr ('strong') and Alsvin ('quick').

He was given a shield named Svalin to protect himself from the heat of the sun. Mani's chariot had one horse. He stole two children from Earth, named Hjuki and Bil, while they were fetching water and made them help him drive the chariot.

Sol and Mani were pursued by wolves, which almost every month caught up and managed to take bites out of the moon.

However, Mani escaped each time and the moon grew back to full size. When Ragnarok approached, the wolves finally caught up and swallowed the sun and moon.

## Sleipnir and Other Horses

Odin's horse Sleipnir was said to be the best of all horses. He had eight legs and could run along the trunk of Yggdrasil to get from one world to another. This ability allowed him to carry Hermod to Helheim in order to request the release of Baldr, and served him well in many stories. How Sleipnir came to be is a rather convoluted tale.

BELOW: Odin's horse Sleipnir was a magical being conceived under very strange circumstances. He fathered several great horses who were associated with mortal heroes, and proved a loyal companion to Odin on his travels.

The walls of Asgard had been destroyed in the Vanir–Aesir war, leaving the home of the gods vulnerable to attack if the Jotnar marched from the direction of Midgard. This was of some concern to the gods, so when a master-builder approached them and offered to build new fortifications, they readily agreed. This may have been a little unwise, since the builder was a Jotunn himself, and he demanded a very high price for his work. This was to be the sun, the moon and the goddess Freya as his wife.

Freya did not like this idea at all, and it seems likely that the gods were opposed to any goddess marrying a Jotunn. There is also the question of whether or not the sun and moon were theirs to give away, and what might have happened if they were forced to try to honour the bargain.

However, Loki suggested that the gods make what amounted to a crooked deal. The builder would receive his desired reward, but only if he could complete the fortification of Asgard by the end of winter without the help of any man.

The builder agreed, despite the fact that this was apparently an impossible task, and set to work. The gods' confidence that they had made a clever bargain soon faded as the work progressed at an incredible rate. The builder did indeed have no help from men but was assisted by a magical stallion named Svadilfari. With the end of winter three days away and the work almost done, the gods realized that they might have to honour their deal. The only option was to find a way to slow down the builder's progress.

The gods turned on Loki, blaming him for the bad deal, and demanded he prevent the completion of the fortifications on time. If he failed, his life would be forfeit. Loki decided that since the stallion was doing most of the work, he needed to be distracted for a time. As the builder and his assistant Svadilfari were out gathering stones to build with, they encountered a mare that the stallion found desirable. This was Loki in disguise, and he led the stallion on a long chase before keeping him occupied for long enough that the building work remained uncompleted.

The walls of Asgard lacked only a few stones around the gates at the end of winter, but the builder had failed in his task and the gods did not need to honour their bargain. They were also released from the oath that they had sworn – that the builder would come to no harm while the work was in progress. Since he was no longer protected, it was safe to kill him and Thor immediately did so.

BELOW: **Sleipnir bore Hermod to Helheim in order to ask for the release of Baldr. Not even the gods could command Hel to release a dead person, though apparently she could do so if she chose.**

Loki, meanwhile, had become pregnant with Svadilfari's foal. This was Sleipnir, whose name translates as 'Sliding (or slippery) One'. He was the best horse among gods and men, and apparently among the Jotnar, too. Odin beat the Jotunn Hrungnir and his horse Gullfaxi in a race with an important prize – the head of the loser.

Sleipnir fathered a line of superior horses. Among them was Grani, the mount of the hero Sigurd. Odin himself helped Sigurd capture Grani and admonished him to take good care of his new horse, for he would become better than any other horse. This is perhaps not surprising, since he was descended from a magical stallion and the Jotunn/Aesir Loki. Since Loki was Odin's adopted brother as well as the mother of his horse, it is possible to think of Sleipnir as Odin's nephew – an indication of just how bizarre the Norse mythos could be.

BELOW: **The appearance of Loki in the form of a mare caused the magical stallion Svadilfari to abandon his work and rush off after her. This resulted in Svadilfari's master failing in his task and forfeiting his life.**

# 5

# THE EDDAS

Most of what is known today about the Norse religion and mythos comes from the Poetic and Prose Eddas, or from the sagas written about mortal heroes and people of note. Much of the accepted body of knowledge about the Norse mythos is inferred from these tales rather than being directly stated.

For example, there are occasions where a being makes definite statements about mythic concepts, such as which god is the father of another, but equally there are many points where a kenning or allusion seems to offer insight into a relationship or situation.

Some of these allusions are contradictory, others confusing. Different poems or tales sometimes reveal entirely different truths – the god Hoenir seems to be quite competent in one tale, but in another he is such a dimwit that he cannot make simple decisions without the counsel of Mimir. Similarly, tales from different regions may feature characters with entirely different names who seem to be the same person, or an individual presented as a god in one tale might be a king or princess in another version. Of course, none of these versions are wrong – each tale is what it is, and it is only in the modern quest for a unified Norse mythos that problems arise.

OPPOSITE: A depiction of Odin from a medieval version of the Eddas. Odin's weapon is anachronistic, appearing more like a falchion than the straight-bladed 'Viking' sword that would be more correctly associated with the Allfather.

## The Poetic Edda

The Poetic Edda, also known as the Elder Edda, is a collection of Norse poems compiled and written down in medieval Iceland. The most important source for these poems is the *Codex Regius*. This was produced in the thirteenth century, but remained obscure until the mid-1600s, when the Bishop of Skalholt, Brynjolfur Sveinsson, procured it. In 1662 he gave it as a gift to the king of Denmark – hence the document's modern name – resulting in its preservation in the Royal Library in Copenhagen until 1971, when it was returned to Iceland.

The Poetic Edda is, as the name suggests, written in alliterative verse. The tales were preserved in oral form for many years before being written down, and verse aids memory as well as providing a form of error checking. If a section does not rhyme, it has probably been misremembered.

THE KENNINGS OF THE POETIC EDDA ARE LESS CONVOLUTED THAN THOSE FOUND IN SKALDIC POETRY.

Using context, vague memories of what the story was supposed to say and a knowledge of rhyme, it is generally possible to reconstruct a forgotten segment. The use of kennings can confound this process, but the kennings used in the Poetic Edda are less convoluted than those found in Skaldic poetry.

## UNDERSTANDING THE OLD NORSE POETRY

The Prose Edda appears to have been created as a guide to the myths, kennings and style used in old Norse poetry, and a narrative version of the stories in the Poetic Edda. It consists of a prologue and three books. The first, *Gylfaginning*, is a compilation of the great Norse myths surrounding the creation of the world and its destruction at Ragnarok. The second, *Skaldskaparmal*, is presented in the form of a conversation between the Norse god of poetry (Bragi) and the Asgard-dwelling Jotunn Aegir. This book contains more myths and stories, but also deals with the nature of poetry and presents a list of kennings. The final book, *Hattatal*, is Sturluson's own creation and is intended as a demonstration of the rules of Norse poetry.

## The Prose Edda

Although known to scholars before the Poetic Edda came to light, the Prose Edda is a more recent creation and is thus sometimes known as the Younger Edda. It is generally believed to have been written by the Icelandic scholar Snorri Sturluson around 1220 AD, although the surviving manuscripts are all later copies. None of them is complete, and there are variations between the surviving versions. The *Codex Regius* is the most complete, with two other medieval manuscripts (*Codex Upsaliensis* and *Codex Wormanius*) also surviving reasonably intact. The *Codex Trajectinus* is a copy made in the 1600s of an older manuscript, and there are also three surviving medieval fragments.

The prologue of the Prose Edda attempts to rationalize the Norse mythos as a distorted history of the ancient world. The individuals identified as Norse gods, according to this account, originated in Troy and used their advanced knowledge to become rulers of primitive northern European tribes. A non-divine Odin took over what is now Germany and established a dynasty, placing his sons as rulers of the Franks, Danes and other peoples. It is stated that the term 'Aesir' comes from 'men of Asia'.

What evidence existed for this rationalization remains unclear, but it was probably done to avoid problems with Christian authorities. At the time the Prose Edda was being written, Christianity was not particularly tolerant of other belief systems. A book about someone else's gods might therefore land the author in trouble, but one that explained pagan beliefs as mere folk tales derived from a misremembered history was much safer to publish – even if it contained the same stories in the main text.

ABOVE: Only a few copies of the Eddas now survive, and then in incomplete form. This is the oldest known copy, dating from long after the end of the 'Viking Age'.

OPPOSITE: In
*Gylfaginning*, Gylfi
addresses his questions
to three beings named as
High, Just-As-High, and
Third. Oddly, High has
the lowest throne, Just-
As-High sits higher, and
Third highest of all.

BELOW: Snorri Sturluson
has been widely
criticised for inventing
parts of his Eddas and
applying Christian
thinking to the Norse
tales. However, without
him we would know
even less about the
Norse mythos.

The first book of the prose Edda, *Gylfaginning* (*The Tricking of Gylfi*), tells how King Gylfi (the earliest known ruler of Sweden) was tricked into accepting the Aesir as gods. These Aesir are the non-divine followers of the mortal Odin described in the prologue to the Prose Edda. Gylfi disguises himself as a man named Gangleri and visits the (mortal) Aesir. He asks them about their religion and is told all about it. This is presented as an attempt by the Aesir to convince Gylfi that they are gods, an approach that allowed Snorri Sturluson to tell the old Norse tales in a way that would keep him out of trouble with the Church authorities.

Sturluson's versions of the Norse myths were reconstructed by him from old poems, and filtered through his mindset as an early Christian scholar. Thus his versions of the myths are incomplete, distorted and in places simply invented. Since much of what we 'know' today about the Norse mythos is derived from these tales, it is probable that what a ninth-century Norseman believed about his gods was not exactly what we think. However, although Sturluson has been criticized for his treatment of the Norse myths, he remains the best source we have, and his work in preserving these ancient tales is both remarkable and praiseworthy.

The second book, *Skaldskaparmal*, may well have been what the Prose Edda was written as a vehicle for. At the time of its creation, the old Norse poetic styles were dying out, largely due to the influence of Christian scholarship. Snorri Sturluson presents these poetic styles and the language they use in a style reminiscent of the Norse poems themselves – a dialogue between Bragi, god of poetry, and Aegir, the Asgard-dwelling Jotunn. The book is to a great extent a guide to the interpretation and creation of poetry in the old Norse styles.

The third book, *Hattatal*, is a demonstration of the various Norse poetic styles. It consists of sections of poetry accompanied by notes on the metre and rules for using alliteration and rhyme. This was Sturluson's attempt to reconstruct the old Norse poetic styles, and he does note that the rules he puts forward were not always followed by old Norse poets. This book was written at a time when the Icelandic language was changing, which might cause many traditions of poetry to be lost or become meaningless to a new generation. Sturluson attempted to preserve the old way by a combination of guides on how to correctly construct a poem and examples of the rules in use.

Snorri Sturluson drew heavily on the poems of the Poetic Edda for his source material, and, despite his attempt to rationalize Norse mythology as the distorted tales of Trojan conquerors, his Prose Edda does follow the poetic versions fairly closely.

## The Poems of the Edda

The Poetic Edda contains a number of poems written in various Norse styles, which preserved the ancient tales of gods, giants and monsters.

### Voluspa

*Voluspa* is the first poem in the Edda, and is the most widely known as it deals with the creation and destruction of the world. A Volva was a seeress; the title of this poem thus translates as 'The Prophecy of the Seeress' (Voluspa). Notably, the seeress begins by asking that the Sons of Heimdall be quiet and listen, referring to humans. This suggests that at one time Heimdall was credited with creating the human race, although later myths clearly ascribe this to Odin. According to Voluspa, the 'sons of Burr' raised the world out of the sea.

ABOVE: This version of the Edda was created in 1666, four centuries after the original creation by Snorri Sturluson. The illustrations are distinctly medieval/renaissance in flavour rather than making any real attempt to preserve the spirit of the original.

Burr (or Borr) was the son of Búri and the father of Odin, so this is clearly a reference to the creation of the world by Odin and his fellows. The poem dwells at length on the creation of the Dwarfs by the gods, listing many of the Dwarfs' names. It relates how the gods lived in peace and happiness until the coming of Gullveig, who practiced her Seidr magic for the Aesir and caused them to go astray. The attempted murder of Gullveig (who was actually the Vanir goddess Freja) triggered the Aesir–Vanir war.

The poem also describes the slaying of Baldr, which was one of the key moments of the Norse myths, since it triggered the chain of events leading to Ragnarok. The Volva tells of the final battle, including the deaths of Odin and Thor, and the rebirth of the world afterwards. She also speaks of how the survivors see the dragon Nidhogg, suggesting that all may not be quite perfect in the renewed world.

## Havamal

*Havamal* is in fact a collection of poems dealing with different subjects. Of these, the first section (*Gestapattr*) is perhaps the most prominent. It consists of wise words attributed to Odin, dealing with interactions between individuals in various circumstances.

Odin's wisdom includes general advice on how to live, stating that although possessions are lost and all mortals die, the one thing that does not fade away is the judgement of a dead man's

life. In short, he is stating that remarkable deeds that win Wordfame are more important than possessions and will live on long after a man's earthly possessions have become meaningless. He states that a nobleman (a 'prince's bairn') should be silent and thoughtful and bold in strife, but also joyous and generous.

A man who seeks the approval of his peers should drink his measure then pass on the ale cup, and speak needful words or not speak at all. Odin advises against overstaying one's welcome and of making mockery of others, even if it seems that no harm can come of it. He also speaks of the dangers of being too trusting. It is an unwise man who assumes that everyone who smiles and flatters him is a friend, Odin warns, but he speaks of the value of friends who treat one another fairly and share gifts and laughter equally among themselves. These gifts need not be great ones; Odin remarks that he won many friends with half a loaf and a tilted jug.

Odin also offers advice on staying alive, including an admonition not to leave weapons behind when travelling, but to

ABOVE: Odin learned much from a Volva, or seeress, who reluctantly told him of his own death and that of Thor at Ragnarok. Knowing that the world would be renewed and that his sons would survive may have provided some comfort.

OPPOSITE: Many of the illustrations of the Eddas show the influence of the Christian world. They were created in the medieval and even renaissance eras, and are often in the style of the time rather than being an accurate representation of the subject matter.

keep them handy in case they are suddenly needed, and advises travellers to spy out a room before entering it in case enemies are lurking. He then moves on to the subject of women, warning of the faithlessness of women in general.

Coming from Odin, this seems a little hypocritical; indeed, in the next stanzas he discusses his attempts to seduce the daughter of Billing, and his successful bid to obtain the Mead of Poetry. In this tale he admits that he used the affections of the mead's guardian, the giantess Gunnlod, to obtain it and paid her back with a poor reward for her affections. This presumably refers to the fact that Odin left her behind to face the wrath of her father Suttung, owner of the mead, as well as any grief their parting might have caused her.

The next section is named *Loddfafnismal*, and puts forward guidelines for living that in many cases echo Odin's earlier statements. He advises men not to take joy in ill news, nor to mock visitors to their hall. Odin states that a man needs friends to whom he can speak the whole of his mind, and is badly off without them – breaking the bonds of friendship will ultimately harm the breaker. However, he does warn that a fickle-tongued flatterer is no friend at all.

Men are wisely admonished not to make shoes or shafts (presumably arrow or spear hafts) for anyone but themselves. A crooked shaft or a defective shoe made for someone else could cause ill feeling. In a wider context, this seems to be an admonition not to take on critical tasks for others, as blame for failure or sub-optimal outcomes might result in enmity or a curse.

In the next section, *Runatal*, Odin recounts how he sought greater wisdom than he already possessed and sacrificed himself to himself, hanging impaled on the tree Yggdrasil for nine nights until the magical runes were revealed to him. He then lists his magical songs, learned from 'the son of Bolthorn'. Bolthorn was father of the primordial Jotunn Bestla, Odin's mother, so this refers to an uncle of Odin who may have been Mimir. Odin proclaims the powers of his songs in this section,

'A MAN SHOULD SPEAK NEEDFUL WORDS OR NOT SPEAK AT ALL.' – *HAVAMAL* which is called *Ljodatal*. His songs can blunt swords, heal the sick, stop arrows in their flight and even reverse a curse so that it falls upon whomever cast it.

## Vafprudnismal

The 'Sayings of Vafprudnir' takes the form of discourse, initially between Odin and Frigg. Having been advised by his wife that Vafprudnir is the most powerful of giants and that Odin's plan to visit him is extremely hazardous, Odin disregards Frigg's advice and makes his way to Vafprudnir's hall.

Disguised and passing himself off as Gagnranor, Odin requests hospitality and then challenges Vafprudnir to a contest to see who is wiser. The loser will forfeit his life. The subsequent questions and answers reveal much about Norse cosmology, such as how the world was created from the body of Ymir and why day and night exist. The two demonstrate their knowledge of the world and its creatures, and the events of Ragnarok, in a lengthy contest before Odin asks a question that Vafprudnir cannot answer.

Odin's question is one that only he would know the answer to: What did Odin whisper in dead Baldr's ear at his funeral? Vafprudnir realizes at this point that his guest is Odin in disguise and that he cannot win the contest. He submits meekly to his fate after naming Odin wisest of the wise.

## Grimnismal

The 'Sayings of Grimnir' is unusual in that it has a large section of prose at the beginning and end. This was probably added much later than the writing of the poem to help the reader understand what is happening. The poem proper consists of a narrative by someone named Grimnir, who is in fact Odin in disguise. Grimnir is being tortured by making him sit between two fires in the hope that he will reveal his identity.

This situation came about as the result of a conversation between Odin and Frigg. The two had previously, for whatever reason, chosen to disguise themselves and look after the children of King Hrauthung. Odin had tutored Geirrod, who became king after his father's death. Frigg's charge, the older brother Agnarr, now lived in a cave.

Odin remarked that his protégé had done rather better than Agnarr, and Frigg responded that Geirrod was not a very good king at all. He was in the habit of torturing his guests if there

BELOW: **Upon realising that he had been torturing the Allfather, King Geirrod leaped up from his seat and accidentally fell on his sword, which had been across his knees. Thus Odin's prophecy that Geirrod's son would become king came true.**

were too many. This was a damning thing to say, as traditional Norse society expected that guests be protected and given the best hospitality possible under the circumstances.

Odin decided to test this assertion, and went in disguise to Geirrod's hall. However, Frigg sent a messenger to warn Geirrod that a magician who wished him ill was on his way, and could be recognized by the fact that no dog would attack him. When Odin arrived he was duly apprehended and made to sit between the two fires. The poem proper begins at this point.

In the poem, Odin (still disguised as Grimnir, and giving no indication to the reader of his identity) delivers a speech about cosmology, the nature of the world and various facts about Odin. He blesses Agnarr, son of Geirrod (confusingly, the son of Geirrod has the same name as Geirrod's older brother, Frigg's protégé) for being the only one to bring him a drink, and states that Agnarr will rule the land of the Goths.

> 'EASY IS IT TO KNOW FOR HIM WHO TO ODIN COMES AND BEHOLDS THE HALL; ITS RAFTERS ARE SPEARS, WITH SHIELDS IS IT ROOFED, ON ITS BENCHES ARE BREASTPLATES STREWN.'
> – GRIMNISMAL

Switching back to prose, the story ends with a revelation that Grimnir is, in fact, Odin. Horrified that he has been torturing the Allfather, Geirrod impales himself on his own sword while trying to free his god, leaving his son to rule as prophesied.

## Skirnismal

The 'Sayings of Skirnir' deals with the occasion where Freyr fell in love with the giantess Gerd. Seeing that his master has become lovesick and miserable, Freyr's servant Skirnir agrees to journey to Jotunheim and ask her to marry Freyr. Upon arriving at the hall of Gerd's father, Skirnir attempts to persuade her into the union. In some versions of this tale she agrees to marry Freyr without coercion, in others she is subjected to dire threats.

Gerd is threatened with being made hideous, and being forced to choose either to live without love or to accept the only partner she will be able to attract – a three-headed giant. Eventually

Gerd agrees to marry Freyr, and plans to meet him in the woods of Barri in nine days. Freyr then laments that waiting a single day will be bad enough, but nine is intolerable.

## Harbardsljod

The 'Lay of Harbaror' is the tale of an encounter between Thor and a ferryman named Harbaror (which translates as 'Greybeard'). It has been theorized that the mysterious ferryman is in fact Loki, but the commonly accepted version is that it is Odin in disguise.

Thor is returning from Jotunheim when he encounters the ferryman, who is unaccountably rude and dismissive towards the god. He insults Thor's dress sense, pretending to have mistaken him for a peasant. Thor issues threats, saying that great trouble will come to the ferryman if he forces Thor to wade across. The ferryman retorts that he is not afraid, and that Thor has not faced a fiercer opponent since he slew the giant Hrungnir.

The two then boast of their exploits in love and war, demanding the other explain what he was doing while wars were being won and giants slain. Thor boasts of how he fought the berserker-women of Hlesey, and Harbaror says this was dishonourable, as harming a woman was forbidden. Thor replies that they were more like she-wolves than women, and his servant was in danger from them.

Harbaror then claims that Thor's wife Sif is unfaithful, and that Thor's wrath might be better spent on her lover. He refuses Thor's demand to bring his boat and give passage, but does agree to tell the god of an alternative – and also both difficult and dangerous – way to get home. Thor departs, threatening to pay the ferryman for the passage he did not grant if they meet again. In return, the ferryman curses him.

As with many of the Norse tales, there seems at first to be no point to this story. However, it serves as a vehicle to recount the great deeds of Thor and Odin; the hurling of insults and baiting of one

BELOW: An Icelandic bronze statue of Thor, who eventually displaced Odin as the primary object of worship. In time, the Norse tales might have evolved to present Thor as the creator of the world and slayer of Ymir.

another is merely a way to set up the narrative contained within the boasts and counter-boasts of each.

## Hymiskvida

'Hymir's Poem' tells the tale of how Thor went fishing for the great serpent Jormungand and stole the giant Hymir's cauldron. This came about as a result of a feast to be prepared by Aegir and Ran, who needed a cauldron or kettle large enough to brew enough mead for all the gods. Aegir was well known for his generosity and the magnificence of his feasts, so this was indeed a very large cauldron. The only one of sufficient size was owned by Hymir, who was not apparently inimical to the gods, but was less friendly than Aegir and Ran.

> TO HIS MISFORTUNE, HYMIR WAS THE OWNER OF THE ONLY CAULDRON LARGE ENOUGH TO BREW ALE FOR ALL THE GODS.

Thor offers to get the cauldron and goes to the abode of Hymir, who is well enough disposed towards Thor that he slaughters three oxen to feed the god while he is staying. However, Hymir had not bargained with Thor's immense appetite; Thor consumes two of the oxen at his first meal, dismaying and annoying Hymir, who states that they will have to go fishing to get more food. He declines to provide Thor with any bait, which proves to be something of a mistake.

Hymir tells Thor to go and find something to use as bait, so Thor chops the head off the greatest of Hymir's oxen. Equipped with this, the two row out to sea and quickly catch two whales. Hymir is pleased, but Thor takes it upon himself to row them far out to sea. Hymir is alarmed, and reminds Thor that his enemy, Jormungand, dwells under this part of the ocean. Thor will not be dissuaded, and casts his line to try to catch the great serpent.

Jormungand takes the bait, and Thor begins to haul the serpent in. Such is the struggle that Thor's feet smash through the bottom of the boat, but he is finally able to pull Jormungand up. He reaches for his hammer to kill it, but Hymir cuts the line out of fear that Thor is about to trigger Ragnarok by slaying his ancient enemy.

Thus Jormungand escapes. Enraged, Thor throws his companion into the sea and rows ashore. As he returns to Aegir's hall he is pursued by a horde of many-headed giants, whom he slays with Mjolnir, described as the 'lover of murder'. Afterwards, the gods are able to have their feast, since Thor kept the kettle and the whales.

## Lokasenna

The poem 'Loki's Quarrel' takes place at another feast hosted by Aegir. Thor is not present, but many of the other gods are. Loki makes himself unwelcome by murdering one of Aegir's servants, apparently out of annoyance at the way he is treating the other gods. Loki is chased off, but sneaks back and forces another servant to reveal what the gods are talking about.

Loki joins the feast, demanding hospitality despite being told he is unwelcome. He is allowed to stay when he invokes an oath made by Odin that they would drink together, but immediately makes trouble. He flings accusations about lack of courage and infidelity around until finally Thor arrives and threatens him until Loki agrees to leave.

There is a section of prose at the end of the poem, detailing how Loki was bound in the cave, but it is not clear from the poem if this happened immediately after the feast or on some other occasion.

ABOVE: A stone carving depicting Thor's fishing expedition with Hymir. Thor was almost successful in catching and killing Jormungand; it is not clear what the consequences would have been.

## Thrymskvida

The 'Lay of Thrym' tells the story of how the Jotunn Thrym stole Mjolnir. It is notable that in this tale Loki helps solve a problem he did not cause, demonstrating that he is a useful – even necessary, for he is instrumental in recovering Mjolnir in this case – member of the Aesir tribe… at least some of the time. Thor wakes to find Mjolnir missing, and is characteristically very angry. After discerning that his hammer is nowhere in the realms of gods or men, Thor asks Loki to help find it, and Loki in turn goes to Freyja. Equipped with her cloak of hawk feathers, Loki flies to Jotunheim and confronts the giant Thrym, who confesses that he has hidden Mjolnir eight miles down in the earth.

Loki returns with news of the hammer's location, and word that Thrym has demanded the goddess Freyja as his wife in return for it. Freyja is not receptive to this idea at all; she becomes so angry that her necklace, Brisingamen, falls from her throat and her hall itself is shaken.

Then Heimdall suggests that a deception is in order. Thor will wear the bridal veil and go to Thrym's palace in Freya's place. Loki will accompany him as a handmaiden. Thor is angered by this idea, saying it would be unmanly for him to wear a wedding dress, but Loki – for once the voice of reason, although perhaps it is more that the idea amuses him – points out that Asgard will be lost to the Jotnar if Mjolnir is not recovered.

Thor does not make a great job of pretending to be a woman. When 'dainties' are presented for the women to eat, the bride downs three tuns of ale and eats an ox as well as eight salmon. Thrym's suspicions are allayed when Loki points out that the bride

'WILT THOU, FREYJA, THY FEATHER-DRESS LEND ME, THAT SO MY HAMMER, I MAY SEEK?' – *THRYMSKVIDA*

was so excited about her wedding that she had not eaten for eight days, and is naturally very hungry.

Thrym then tries to kiss his prospective bride, but is dissuaded by Thor's blazing, angry eyes. Again, Loki is forced to explain. This time he claims that the bride has not slept for eight nights, so great is her excitement. Thrym buys this lame excuse, too, and calls for Mjolnir to be brought into the hall. It is given to the bride to hallow the wedding, and placed upon her lap. Thor blessed many weddings with his hammer, but not this one. As soon as Mjolnir is within reach, he begins slaying everything in sight. After killing Thrym and his kin, Thor and Loki return to Asgard with Mjolnir.

RIGHT: Whilst searching for his Valkyrie wife Volund was robbed of his treasures, hamstrung and imprisoned by King Nithuth. He took a terrible vengeance upon the family of his captor.

OPPOSITE: The wise Dwarf Alviss courts Thor's daughter, Thrud.

## Volundarkvida

'The Lay of Volund' appears to have its origins in Germanic myths dating from before the 'Viking Age', and may have originated outside Scandinavia. Much of the surviving text is extremely hard to read, making reconstruction of the poem a problem.

Volund, who is at one point referred to as belonging to the race of Elves, is a great craftsman who comes upon three Valkyries while hunting with his two brothers. Each brother marries one of the Valkyries, of whom at least two are daughters of kings. They dwell together happily for seven years, after which the Valkyries fly away to return to their duties. Each brother follows his wife; Volund sets off on snowshoes after his wife Olrun, but is captured by Nithuth, a Swedish king.

Nithuth takes from Volund the treasures he has made, and even his sword, and hamstrings him. Volund is incarcerated on an island and forced to work for Nithuth, while the ring he made for his Valkyrie bride is given to Nithuth's daughter Bothvild. Volund begins his revenge by enticing the sons of Nithuth with gold and gems, then killing them and fashioning gifts for Nithuth from their body parts. He seduces Bothvild before revealing to Nithuth what he has done to the king's children.

## The Lays of Helgi Hjorvardsson

There are three sections of the Poetic Edda that deal with the life of Helgi Hjorvardsson, and a great deal of controversy surrounding all of them. The original story may have come from Denmark; there is some evidence that Helgi may have been the son of King Halfdan. It has become distorted over time, and the surviving text is fragmentary and difficult to reconstruct. As a result, a number of scholars have quite different theories about these stories. The first tale begins with the early life of Helgi, which was laid out by the Norns who

## ALVISSMAL

This poem is a discourse between the wise Dwarf Alviss (hence the poem's name, 'Alviss-talk') and Thor. Alviss claims that Thor's daughter Thrud is promised to him in marriage, which Thor refutes, but in a gambit more likely to be associated with Odin than Thor, he agrees that Alviss can marry his daughter if he can answer Thor's questions about the cosmos.

Thor's questions are all about what the various different groups of beings call the same object. It turns out that the Elves, the Dwarfs, the Jotnar, the gods and humans all have different names for the moon, the sun, the sky and other cosmological bodies. Essentially, Alviss' answers are a guide to some of the kennings used by Skaldic poets.

In the end, Alviss' wisdom is for naught; Thor keeps him talking until the sun comes up and its rays turn the Dwarf to stone. This is out of character for Thor, who would normally chase off an unwanted suitor with angry shouts, or perhaps simply kill him on the spot.

came to visit him as an infant. His heroic nature is established when he slays Hunding and then refuses to make recompense to Hunding's sons. This results in conflict and the death of the sons as well. He then helps the Valkyrie Sigrun, who has been promised in marriage to an unworthy prince. Helgi defeats Sigrun's betrothed and marries her instead.

In another story, Helgi meets a Valkyrie called Svafa. At this time he does not have a name, and it is she that names him Helgi. Svafa reveals to Helgi the location of a magical sword that can destroy the shields of enemies, and provides him with assistance in battle. He then becomes a famous hero, slaying kings and giants, and marries Svafa. This is another tale where a Jotunn is turned into stone by the sun's rays.

## HELGI IS TAKEN TO VALHOL AND ASKED TO LEAD THE EINHERJAR.

In this tale, Helgi meets his end after encountering a giantess, who appears to be the supremely strong Hyrokkin, and offending her. Cursed by the giantess, he is mortally wounded in a duel. At the end of the poem it is stated that Svafa and Helgi are to be reincarnated, and the third of the Lays of Helgi carries on from this. It appears to be parts of several ancient poems collected together and has a similar story to the first, with a different version of the slaying of Hunding.

Helgi meets the Valkyrie Sigrun (who is Svafa reincarnated) and again helps her avoid an unwelcome marriage by defeating the prince to whom she has been betrothed. The two marry and have children, but Helgi is betrayed by Dagr, Sigrun's brother. With the assistance of a spear loaned by Odin, who seems to want Helgi as a warrior for Valhol, Dagr slays Helgi and is cursed by his sister.

Helgi is taken to Valhol, as befits a great warrior, and is asked by Odin to lead the Einherjar. He is sent back to the mortal world from time to time, and even spends a night in his barrow with Sigrun. He never returns to her after this, and she eventually dies of grief. The two are reincarnated again – he as another hero named Helgi and she as the Valkyrie Kara.

Helgi's sagas are followed by a section of prose entitled *Fra Dauda Sinfjotla*, or 'On the Death of Sinfjotli'. It deals with the

LEFT: **It is possible that Helgi and his Valkyrie wife Sigrun were reunited in Valhol as depicted here. Other versions of their tale have them both reincarnated to meet again in the mortal world.**

death by poisoning of Sinfjotli, son of Sigmund and half-brother to Helgi and Sigurd. Sinfjotli had killed the brother of Borghild, his father's wife, in a quarrel over a woman. Serving ale at a feast, Borghild poisons Sinfjotli's drink. He realizes this and at first refuses to drink, but ultimately does and is killed. The Volsung Saga, found in the Prose Edda, provides a more coherent version of at least some of the events surrounding the life of Helgi, and also the characters in the following poems.

## The Lays of Sigurd, Gudrun and Brynhild

Sigurd, who appears in Germanic legend as Siegfried, is the slayer of the dragon Fafnir. His tale is told in prose form in the Prose Edda, and appears in the form of several poems in the Poetic Edda. The first of these is *Gripisspa*, sometimes called the 'First Lay of Sigurd, Fafnir's Slayer'. Like many poems of the Edda, *Gripisspa* takes the form of a conversation, this time between Sigurd (the son of Sigmund and future dragon slayer) and his

RIGHT: **After accidentally imbibing some of Fafnir's blood, Sigurd found himself able to understand the speech of birds. He was thus warned against the treachery of Regin, his foster-father and the instigator of his dragon-slaying mission.**

uncle Gripir. Gripir predicts the events of Sigurd's life, essentially giving the reader an outline of the events related in several other poems. Although chronologically these events occur first, the poem is a late addition to the collection found in the Edda.

*Gripisspa* is followed by an untitled section that is often considered to be one rather fragmented poem, but given that the poetic style changes, it may be a compilation of more than one. The section is normally referred to as *Reginsmal* ('Regin's Sayings'), or as the 'Second Lay of Sigurd, Fafnir's Slayer'. Poetry and prose sections first deal with how Loki slew Otr and obtained the cursed ring Andvarinaut as part of his weregild, thus passing it to King Hreidmar whose son Fafnir then went mad with greed. The later part of the poem is about Sigurd and his foster-father Regin.

The next section, again untitled, but normally referred to as *Fafnismal* ('Fafnir's Sayings'), deals with the slaying of Fafnir by Sigurd and the subsequent betrayal of Sigurd by his foster-father Regin. Able to understand the speech of birds due to accidentally drinking some of Fafnir's blood, Sigurd learns of Regin's treachery in time to save himself. The birds also tell him of the Valkyrie Brynhild and Sigurd's future wife, Gudrun (or Guthrun).

The next section is also untitled, but is usually called *Sigrdrifumal*. Sigurdrifa translates as 'Bringer of Victory' and is used to refer to the Valkyrie Brynhild, whose advice to Sigurd makes up much of the text. Brynhild teaches Sigurd about the use of runic magic in this section of the Edda, making it one of the most important sources on the subject. However, the end of the section is lost from the *Codex Regius*, which has a gap of several leaves known as the 'Great Lacuna'. Some of the text has been reconstructed from other surviving versions of the Poetic Edda.

The missing section of the *Codex Regius* contained the first part of an extremely long poem named *Brot af Sigurdarvida* ('The Lay of Sigurd'), which may have contained the entire saga of Sigurd. There appear to have been both a short 'Lay of Sigurd' (which was not all that short, at about 70 stanzas) and a long 'Lay of Sigurd', which may have had as many as 250.

The events of the missing section can be filled in from the prose of the Volsung Saga, which appears in the Prose Edda.

Essentially, Sigurd meets Brynhild's brother-in-law, after which a woman named Gudrun visits Brynhild to ask about the meaning of a dream she has had. Brynhild explains the dream with a prophecy of what is about to happen.

Sigurd then visits the home of Gudrun and her brother Gunnar, where their mother gives Sigurd a magical draught that makes him forget about Brynhild. He marries Gudrun and agrees to help Gunnar win Brynhild as his bride. Brynhild is surrounded by a ring of flames, which Gunnar cannot pass. Sigurd is disguised as Gunnar to make Brynhild think that Gunnar was the one who rescued her, and spends three nights with the Valkyrie.

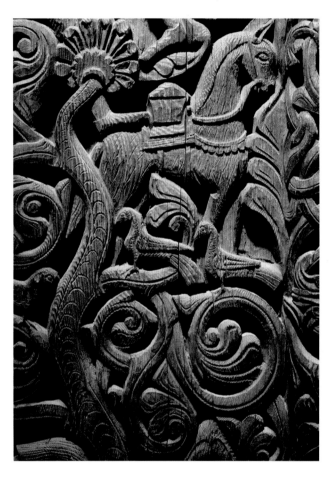

ABOVE: **Brynhild was surrounded by a wall of flames, through which no man save heroic Sigurd could pass. He did so in disguise as his blood-brother Gunnar to win Brynhild as Gunnar's wife.**

Some versions of the story have Sigurd 'laying his sword between them', while others state that Brynhild gives herself to Sigurd while he is disguised as Gunnar. Either way, Brynhild's wedding preparations are interrupted by a quarrel with Gudrun, during which she discovers that it was Sigurd who rescued her, rather than Gunnar. Brynhild's anger cannot be calmed by either Gunnar or Sigurd, and the latter is grief stricken when he discovers what has happened. He is so upset that his mail-coat is burst asunder. Meanwhile, Gunnar plots vengeance against Sigurd.

Sigurd is slain by Gunnar and his men somewhere 'south of the Rhine'. Gudrun curses Gunnar for what he has done, and Brynhild foretells disaster for Gunnar, for he is now an oath-breaker and a kinslayer. She says that Sigurd, who was Gunnar's blood brother, would have been the greatest of men had he lived much longer. Brynhild tells Gudrun that she should kill herself and follow Sigurd into the afterlife, as Brynhild intends to do.

However, she foretells that Gudrun will not commit suicide, but will have sons with another man.

## Lays of Gudrun

In the first of the three 'Lays of Gudrun' (*Gudrunarkvida I, II and III*), Sigurd's wife Gudrun laments his death. Various people try to console Gudrun by explaining that they, too, have suffered great loss and managed to get on with their lives, but to no avail. This is followed by a section of prose in which Gudrun travels to Denmark and remains there for some time. Brynhild kills herself with a sword after ordering several of her servants put to death. She had already ordered Sigurd to be accompanied on his funeral pyre by killed slaves, dogs and hawks, and that the door to the

ABOVE: Some versions of the tale have Sigurd rather unheroically murdered in his sleep by Gunnar's men. This made Gunnar an oath-breaker as well as a kin slayer, as he had sworn brotherly loyalty to Sigurd.

afterlife be left open behind him until he had been joined by this retine and Brynhild herself.

'Brynhild's Hell-Ride' (*Helreid Brynhildar*) tells of the funerals of Sigurd and Brynhild. Although Brynhild ordered Sigurd's pyre to be wide enough for two, her body is burned separately to and after his. On her way to the afterlife she encounters a giantess and explains how recent events are not entirely her fault. She was captured by a king when very young, along with her sisters. Later she offended Odin by giving victory in battle to King Agnar (who may have been her captor), causing the death of King Hjalmgunnar whom Odin had favoured.

For this offence Brynhild was imprisoned within a ring of fire and made to sleep until a brave man could rescue her. Her saviour was Sigurd, in disguise as his blood-brother Gunnar. Brynhild points out that she was deceived by others, suggesting that the blame is not hers. She finally states that although men and women suffer throughout their lives on Earth, she and Sigurd will be together in the afterlife.

LEFT: The image of the Valkyrie (in this case Brynhild) bearing a fallen warrior to Valhol has become the popular conception of their role. Certainly this version is far more romantic than a horde of carrion-beasts descending upon the corpses of the slain.

'Brynhild's Hell-Ride' is followed by a prose section named *Drap Nuflinga* ('Slaying of the Niflungs'). This appears to be part of an attempt to create a more coherent narrative by inserting links and explanations between the poetic sections. In *Drap Niflunga*, Gudrun's second husband, Atli, kills her brothers Gunnar and Hogni.

Atli is Brynhild's brother and blames Gudrun's family for her death. In recompense he demands Gudrun as his wife. She is given the same magical draught that had caused Sigurd to forget about Brynhild and marry Gudrun, and is wedded to Atli. Whether or not the draught of forgetfulness worked is doubtful. Gudrun detects Atli's plan to murder her brothers and tries to warn them. This is to no avail; Hogni's heart is cut out and his brother Gunnar is cast into a pit of adders where a snake bites him in the liver.

# IN RECOMPENSE FOR THE DEATH OF HIS SISTER BRYNHILD, ATLI DEMANDS THAT GUDRUN BECOMES HIS WIFE.

'The Second Lay of Gudrun' has the same title as the first (*Gudrunarkvida*) in the original text, but is normally entitled *Gudrunarkvida II* in order to differentiate it. Although the surviving text has some pieces missing this is still one of the most

RIGHT: Gudrun's stories are a series of laments for the increasing number of relatives and husbands who are slain around her. The death of her husband Sigurd is the first of her many woes.

complete ancient poems to be found. It is older than the 'First Lay', dating from some time before 1000 AD, and has similar content for the most part. Gudrun laments the death of Sigurd (as in the first), but also the murder of her brothers at the hands of Atli. The latter dreams of the death of his own two sons, whose flesh is served to him by Gudrun.

'The Third Lay of Gudrun' also has the same title as the others, but is normally referred to as *Gudrunarkvida III* for clarity. It appears to have originated in Germany, and may not have been known in Scandinavia at the time the Volsung Saga was being written. It is essentially a traditional Germanic tale in which a wife is accused of adultery and proves her innocence by undergoing an ordeal by boiling water. This required that she pick a stone out of a kettle of boiling water, which typically would be wrist-deep, but might be much deeper in some cases. If, after three days, the injuries inflicted in the process were healing well, innocence was proven.

*Gudrunarkvida III* seems to be a retelling of this traditional tale with Gudrun, Atli and other well-known characters of the time added in place of the original subjects. In this case Herkja, a former concubine of Atli, tells him that she has seen Gudrun with King Thjothrek. Gudrun swears that she was not unfaithful; she and the visiting king were merely sharing tales of their lost followers and loved ones. She declares that she wishes to avenge her brothers, and demands the ordeal of boiling water. Gudrun's hand comes out from the water uninjured, after which Herkja has to perform the same task. She is badly burned, proving her testimony to be false, and is thrown into a bog to drown.

'The Lament of Oddrun', or *Oddrunargratr*, seems to be drawn from Germanic legend and is probably a late addition to the story of Sigurd and Gudrun. Oddrun is Atli's sister and the lover of Gunnar, brother of Gudrun. The poem tells the tale of how Oddrun helped Borgny, daughter of Heithrek, but was powerless when Gunnar and his brother Hogni were murdered by Atli. Oddrun's skill at healing is not sufficient to save her lover after he is bitten by an adder.

ABOVE: Text of the 'Song of Gudrun' from the Poetic Edda. Several versions of Gudrun's laments exist, probably added to over time as the story was extended and embellished.

# THE LAYS OF ATLI

There are two poems in the *Codex Regius* about Atli, who appears to be a character derived from Attila the Hun. The shorter of the two is *Atlakvitha* ('Lay of Atli'); the longer is *Atlamol* ('Ballad of Atli'). Both tell more or less the same story, but *Atlamol* adds additional details and embellishments. These poems have become associated with Greenland and may well have been written in one of the settlements there.

'The Lays of Atli' tell the story of how Atli murdered Gudrun's brothers and is then slain by Gudrun. The details are similar to other versions of the tale. Atli summons the brothers to his hall with the offer of riches. The brothers are suspicious since they are already very wealthy, and Gudrun also manages to send a warning. Nevertheless, the brothers come to Atli's hall and are captured. Atli demands that they tell him where their gold is hidden, but they will not. Both are put to death.

Atli then feasts with his men, and Gudrun serves food and drink. During the feast she tells Atli that he has been eating the hearts of his sons and later, when he is drunk in bed, she kills him. After giving away Atli's gold and freeing his thralls, she burns down his hall for good measure.

# *Guthrunarhvot* and *Hamthesmol*

*Guthrunarhvot* ('Guthrun's Inciting') and *Hamthesmol* ('The Ballad of Hamther') have very similar subject matter. The events of the poems result from the actions of King Jormunrekr. The latter was a king of the Goths whose name has been translated into many forms. Also known as Ermanaric and Eormenric, he was warlike and cruel. The tale of how he put a woman named Sunilda to death in a sadistic manner, after which a revenge attempt was made against him, has been told in various forms throughout northern Europe. It seems to have been incorporated into the Norse mythos using characters from other tales in place of the original victim and her relatives.

According to this version, Guthrun (Gudrun) had a daughter with Sigurd. This woman, who was named Svanhild, married King Jormunrekr. Jormunrekr discovered that his son Randver was having an affair with his wife, and had her either trampled to death or pulled apart by horses, depending on the version of the legend. Gudrun obtained vengeance by sending her sons Hamdir and Sorli to kill Jormunrekr.

The surviving text of these poems is fragmentary, and it is quite likely that they were not written in their current form, but instead pieced together by an earlier writer from extant material. *Hamthesmol* is referred to as the 'Old Ballad of Hamther' and may have been used as a source when creating *Guthrunarhvot*. The story is the same but *Hamthesmol* is more of a straight telling of the tale, whereas much of *Guthrunarhvot* is yet another lament by Guthrun (Gudrun) for Sigurd and everyone else who has died so far in her tragic life.

In *Hamthesmol*, Guthrun tells her sons of the murder of their sister and bids them take vengeance. The sons know that this is a death-ride, but agree to try anyway. Guthrun proclaims that the two of them will slay 200 Goth warriors in their fortress. The poem is fragmented, with several parts missing, but other sources suggest that Guthrun had somehow contrived to make the heroes' armour impenetrable to weapons. She counsels them not to touch stones or other heavy things as this will undo the magic.

Hamther and Sorli meet their half-brother Erp on the road. He offers to help them as one hand or foot helps another, but for reasons that are unclear in the poem they slay him instead. After this, both brothers suffer falls and misfortunes that force them to save themselves using hand and foot, and they realize they have done a terrible deed and robbed themselves of a third warrior.

Nevertheless, Hamdir and Sorli storm the burg of Jormunrekr while his warriors are feasting, arriving unexpectedly and quickly overwhelming the guards. When he hears of the attack, Jormunrekr boasts that he will capture and hang the heroes. He orders his men to hurl stones at the brothers, since steel will not bite them. In the Prose Edda this insight comes from Odin, who arrives in the guise of an old man and tells the king how to defeat these invincible Goth-slayers.

**OPPOSITE:** As prophesied by Brynhild, Gudrun did not slay herself out of grief, but instead was forced to marry King Atli, Brynhild's brother. This resulted in the death of Atli and the destruction of his hall.

**BELOW:** Odin warns King Jormunrekr (Ermanaric) that the two warriors' armour is impervious to iron and advises the Goths to throw stones at them instead of using their swords.

Hamther and Sorli realize they are undone and lament their mistakes – notably the slaying of their half-brother. They state that their Wordfame will be great for this deed, for they have fought a great battle against tremendous odds. After stating that nobody can defy his fate the brothers are killed in the final stanza.

*Guthrunarhvot* revolves around the same incident, and indeed the first part of the poem is very similar. The remainder consists of Guthrun lamenting everyone that has been killed around her. The poem finishes with the hope that everyone suffers a bit less in the future, or perhaps that Guthrun's tale of disaster and woe might make others' suffering seem a little less severe.

## The Sagas

Numerous Norse sagas exist, not all of which deal with religious or mythical matters except perhaps in passing. The sagas of kings, bishops and of Icelanders are historical in nature, and while they may refer at times to religious matters, they are not mythic tales in their own right. Some of the sagas mix mortals and gods or monsters, and illustrate or draw upon the Norse myths.

By way of example, in Egil's Saga, the hero Egil uses a Nithing-pole (a rune-carved pole with a severed horse's head atop it) to curse the land spirits until they turn against his enemies. Egil Skallagrimsson was not a mythical hero; he is presented as a real person who interacts with known historical figures, and many modern Icelanders count him among their ancestors. This blurring of the line between historical reality and mythical stories has been referred to as 'heroic (or mythic) history', often showing known real people involved in events that are straight out of myth.

The Volsung Saga is particularly relevant since it tells the same tale as much of the Poetic Edda, although in more coherent form, and involves several interventions by Odin. The story

BELOW: Pendants depicting Norse heroes, part of a large Viking hoard from the year 1000 AD. According to 'Odin's law' as narrated in the Eddas, treasure hidden in this life would be available in the next.

probably originated in central Europe before the 'Viking Age' and made its way through Germanic lands into Scandinavia. A very similar Germanic version can be found in the *Nibelungenlied*. As presented in the Prose Edda, the Volsung Saga features characters who also appear in tales of the gods. Fafnir and his family are here presented as humans – although quite magical ones it seems – rather than Dwarfs.

## The Volsung Saga

The Volsung Saga parallels many of the events told of in the Poetic Edda, but in narrative prose form. It begins with an incident where a son of Odin named Sigi murdered his thrall Bredi in a jealous rage and was outlawed. Odin's patronage of outlaws is evident here – he showed him where to find ships and men, and thus permitted Sigi to become a king.

Sigi's son Rerir was even greater, but his wife could not conceive until the gods sent her a magical apple. She was then pregnant for six years and died after giving birth to a son named Volsung. Volsung was another great king, whose many children included Sigmund and his sister Signy. She was promised in marriage, against her wishes, to King Siggeir of Gautland.

In the hall of King Volsung was a tree named Barnstock. A mysterious stranger – who was almost certainly Odin – came to the hall and thrust a sword

BELOW: Odin plunged a magical sword into the tree Barnstock. Only Sigmund could remove it, so it became his property. The sword was coveted by King Siggeir, but Sigurd would not sell it, beginning a tragic chain of events.

into the tree, saying it belonged to whomever could pull it out. Nobody could do so until Sigmund tried; he found it easy. King Siggeir decided he wanted the sword and offered gold for it, but Sigmund declined.

Siggeir began to plot revenge for this refusal, and invited Volsung and his family to visit him. They did so, and despite a warning from Signy, the visitors were attacked. Volsung was killed and his sons captured, including Sigmund. They were placed in stocks to be harried by wild animals, and one by one they were killed until only Sigmund remained. Aided by Signy he escaped to live in the woods.

## VOLSUNG AND HIS MEN WERE DEFEATED, AND VOLSUNG'S SONS WERE ALL CAPTURED.

Signy had two sons by her husband Siggeir, and in their youth she tested their courage with the aid of Sigmund. They were found lacking so Sigmund killed them. Signy then swapped shapes with a sorceress, who slept with King Siggeir while Signy visited her brother Sigmund. The two became lovers and Signy eventually gave birth to a son, who she named Sinfjotli. Siggeir thought the boy was his and raised him. When sent to Sigmund to assess his courage, he passed the test. Sigmund took him hunting and raiding.

On one of their expeditions, Sigmund and Sinfjotli stole wolfskins and could not remove them for a time, running wild as animals and fighting each other. Sinfjotli was almost killed, but was saved by a magical leaf delivered by a raven. These adventures served to toughen the boy to the point where he was willing to kill his own family members. When he and Sigmund sneaked into Siggeir's estate to seek revenge, they were spotted by two other children that Signy had by Siggeir. Signy brought the children to Sigmund and advised him to kill them, but he refused.

Sinfjotli immediately slew the children and took their bodies to King Siggeir. He and Sigmund then attacked the king, but were captured. They were buried alive inside a mound, but escaped when Signy brought Sigmund his sword inside a bundle of straw. They then set Siggeir's hall afire and announced that the Volsungs were not all dead after all. Signy chose to stay and die with King Siggeir, while Sigmund and Sinfjotli returned to Volsung's kingdom.

In time, Sigmund married a woman named Borghild. Together they had sons named Hamund and Helgi. The latter was prophesied by the Norns to one day be the greatest king of all. In the interim, he honed his skills in raiding, and along the way encountered a woman named Sigrun who was to marry King Hodbrodd. She did not want to, and asked Helgi to fight for her. Accompanied by Sinfjotli, Helgi brought his army to fight Hodbrodd; Sinfjotli exchanged insults with Hodbrodd's father and made sure that there would be a fight.

During the battle, Helgi's warriors were aided by a force of shieldmaidens (presumably Valkyries) and defeated Hodbrodd. He claimed Hodbrodd's kingdom for his own and married Sigrun. After this point, Helgi played no further part in the Volsung saga, but Sinfjotli continued raiding and so encountered a woman who

BELOW: Sigmund's sword broke on the shaft of Odin's spear. Dying, he realized that Odin wanted the weapon to pass on to someone else and ordered the pieces be kept for his unborn son.

was also desired by the brother of King Sigmund's wife Borghild. Sinfjotli killed him in a duel.

When Sigmund refused to exile her brother's slayer, Borghild poisoned him. Sinfjotli knew of the trick and tried to avoid drinking, but his father Sigmund rather unwisely advised him to drink, and Sinfjotli drank. He died, and Sigmund took his body to a nearby fjord where he encountered a mysterious ferryman who was almost certainly Odin. The ferryman offered to take them across the fjord, but said that there was no room in the boat for three. He took Sinfjotli's body and left Sigmund behind; he did not return.

## ODIN GIFTED THE YOUNG SIGURD WITH GRANI, THE GREATEST OF HORSES.

Sigurd banished Borghild, who then died, and eventually married a princess named Hjordis. She had to choose between Sigmund, who was very old at the time, and King Lyngvi, who was angered at Sigmund and attacked his army. During their battle, a one-eyed man in a hooded cloak, armed with a spear, attacked Sigmund. This was, of course, Odin, against whose magical spear the sword of Sigmund – given to him by Odin himself – shattered. Sigmund's army was defeated and he was wounded.

The dying Sigmund told his wife Hjordis that he knew she was pregnant, and that it was obvious Odin did not want him to have the magical sword any longer. It would be reforged and named Gram, and given to their son when he was in need of it. After Sigmund died, Hjordis was captured by Viking raiders who took her to their ruler, King Alf. Alf heard her tale and offered to marry her, raising her son as his own.

The boy was named Sigurd, and in the tradition of the Norsemen he was fostered to Hreidmar's son Regin. Regin taught him how to read the runes and to speak the languages of foreign people, and one day Odin came to Sigurd with a gift. This was a young horse who Sigurd named Grani. Odin bade him look after the animal, for he was of Sleipnir's kin and would be the greatest of horses.

Later, Regin told Sigurd of how his own father, Hreidmar, was murdered by Regin's brother Fafnir. Their third brother Otr

was killed by the god Loki while fishing in the shape of an otter. Hreidmar demanded weregild in compensation for his son's life, and Loki brought him a cursed ring he had taken from the Dwarf Andvari. Fafnir had gone mad with greed and stolen all the treasure. He had turned into a dragon to guard it and now terrorized the countryside.

Sigurd asked Regin, who was trained as a smith, to forge him a sword with which to slay the dragon. His early attempts were not good enough; they shattered when Sigurd struck the anvil with them. Then Sigurd brought the broken pieces of the sword Gram to Regin, and when this blade was reforged it cut right through the anvil.

Sigurd then spoke to his mother's brother Gripir, who could see the future. Gripir told him that he must avenge Sigurd before he went after Fafnir, so he took a force of men and ships against King Lyngvi and slew him. Afterwards, Regin accompanied Sigurd on his expedition against the dragon Fafnir, but fled after advising Sigurd on how to kill the beast. As Sigurd was digging a trench to ambush the dragon, an old man with a long beard – Odin again – advised him to add more trenches to allow Fafnir's blood to drain away and not drown him.

ABOVE: A runestone depicting the hero Sigurd with his magical sword Gram. With this weapon he slew both the dragon Fafnir and the traitorous Regin.

Sigurd fatally stabbed the dragon Fafnir and spoke with him as he died. Fafnir advised leaving the treasure, but Sigurd took it, along with Fafnir's heart and some of his blood. This he gave to Regin, cooking the heart for him to eat. However, Sigurd had swallowed some of the blood and now understood the speech of birds. He was thus forewarned of Regin's intent to betray him and beheaded the traitor with his sword Gram.

After securing the dragon's hoard, Sigurd followed the advice of the birds and came to a mountain where the Valkyrie Brynhild slept, surrounded by a ring of fire. She knew who he was when he woke her, and explained that she was imprisoned as a punishment for defying Odin. She then taught Sigurd how to use the runes to make magic.

Sigurd left Brynhild and went to the estate of Heimir, who was married to Brynhild's sister, and Brynhild later arrived there. However, she refused his advances, saying that he was destined to marry Gudrun, daughter of King Gjuki. Gudrun came to see

Brynhild to ask her what a recent and very unpleasant dream meant. Brynhild foretold what was to happen next, which was upsetting to Gudrun.

Later, Sigurd arrived at the hall of King Gjuki, where Gjuki's wife Grimhild used a magical ale of forgetfulness to make him forget Brynhild. He married Gudrun and swore blood-brotherhood with her brothers Gunnar, Hogni and Guttorm. They had a son whom they named Sigmund.

Gunnar was urged by his mother to ask Brynhild to marry him, but she did not want to wed and fortified herself behind a wall of flames to keep potential suitors out. She swore that she would marry only the man who could break through this wall. After Gunnar failed despite Sigmund's help, Sigmund disguised himself as Gunnar and reached Brynhild. They spent three nights together, although Sigmund's unsheathed sword lay between them in the bed. Sigmund also took the magical ring Andvarinaut from her and gave her another.

Gunnar and Brynhild, who had not spotted the deception, were married. However, Gudrun and Brynhild did not get along and began to quarrel about whose husband was the best. Gudrun cited Sigurd's slaying of Fafnir

BELOW: **Sigurd's marriage to Gudrun was facilitated by a draught of forgetfulness. This caused him to forget about Brynhild, who had previously refused to marry him. Gudrun's boasting eventually revealed how Brynhild had been deceived.**

and trumped all of Brynhild's arguments by revealing that it was Sigurd, not Gunnar, who rescued her.

Brynhild resented what she saw as a betrayal, and incited Gunnar to kill Sigurd. He could not do so, since he was bound by oaths of brotherhood, and nor could his brother Hogni. Their younger brother Guttorm was not so bound, and was sent to kill Sigurd in his sleep. As he fled, the mortally wounded Sigurd hurled his sword and cut Guttorm in two. Hearing Gudrun's grief, Brynhild was overcome with remorse and killed herself after requesting that she share Sigurd's funeral pyre.

Gudrun then went away and was lost for seven and a half years before her family found her. They had promised King Atli (Brynhild's brother) that Gudrun would marry him in recompense for Brynhild's death. Atli wanted Fafnir's gold for himself, and reasoned that Gudrun's brothers would know where it was. He invited them to his hall, and they came despite a warning from Gudrun. This was altered by a treacherous servant so that the runes no longer warned of Atli's betrayal.

Although the runic deception was spotted, the brothers went to Atli's hall anyway, and Atli demanded they reveal the location of Fafnir's gold. They refused, and fought all of Atli's guards assisted by Gudrun, who joined her brothers wearing a borrowed mail-coat. They were eventually overpowered and Hogni was slain by having his heart cut out. Gunnar still defied Atli, saying that he alone knew where the treasure was, and he would not reveal his secret. He was cast into a snake pit where he survived for a time by playing a harp

## GUDRUN FOUGHT ALONGSIDE HER BROTHERS AGAINST ATLI'S MEN, WEARING A BORROWED MAIL-COAT.

(given to him by Gudrun) with his feet. However, although the snakes were mostly put to sleep by the harp, one bit him.

Gudrun took revenge on Atli by killing the two sons they had together and putting their blood in his wine, and then serving their hearts to him in a feast. Together with Niflung, a son of Hogni who had survived the battle against Atli, Gudrun set fire to Alti's hall and stabbed him through the chest. So ended the saga of the Volsungs.

# 6

# RAGNAROK

The old Norse religion contained several, sometimes conflicting, versions of what happened to people after they died. There was no simple division between those who lived a good life and those who did not; that would not be in keeping with the nature of Norse beliefs that were far less black-and-white than those of monotheistic cultures.

Warriors who died heroically in battle could expect to be taken by Valkyries to await the day of Ragnarok as Einherjar – fighters reborn. Half went to Odin's hall at Valhol and half to Folkvangr. Both places were apparently similar, although since Odin was the lord of Valhol and Freyja ruled Folkvangr there may have been some differences between the two.

Within Valhol, food was provided by the beast Saehriminir, which could be killed and eaten each night and returned to life to provide more food the next day. This was prepared by Andhrimnir, who had a cauldron named Eldhrimnir. Atop the roof of Valhol stood the goat Heidrun, who produced a constant stream of mead, and the hart Eikthyrinr, from whose antlers dripped water that refilled the Well of Hvergelmir. Both fed from

OPPOSITE: At Ragnarok, many of the gods fought against their greatest enemies to mutual destruction. Thor was destined to slay and be slain by the great serpent Jormungand. He lived just long enough to know he had won the fight.

the tree Laerad, which grew close to Odin's hall. This tree is usually associated with Yggdrasil, and may be the site of Odin's self-sacrifice when he gained the power of the runes.

Within the hall of Valhol, the chosen warriors feasted all night and drank mead served by Valkyries. During the day they engaged in endless combat to ready them for Valhol. Those who were killed, maimed or even chopped asunder during combat were renewed each night. However, not everyone in Valhol was pleased with his fate it seems. The hero Helgi was brought to Valhol upon his death, and Odin asked him to help rule it. This was presumably pleasing to Helgi, who the Norns had said would be a great king, but less so for his old enemy Hunding. Hunding had presumably died well when Helgi fought him, since he was in Valhol, but nevertheless Helgi made him look after the animals and wash the feet of the weary Einherjar.

Folkvangr, which translates as 'field of the host' or 'field of the people', was a land or meadow wherein lay Freyja's hall Sessrumnir. Less is known about Folkvangr, although the general purpose of Folkvangr was much the same as Valhol. Freya herself may have been a Valkyrie, since she is noted as choosing half

BELOW: **After a day of battling one another, with many casualties, the Einherjar enjoyed an evening of feasting and drinking. Their wounds were magically healed, as presumably was any mead-induced hangover the next morning.**

the slain each day of battle. It is possible to interpret the relevant passages as meaning that Freyja gets first choice of those to be taken to Valhol or Folkvang, ahead of Odin, but why this would be is unclear unless she was in charge of the selection process as a Valkyrie.

## Battle of Hjadningavig

Freyja also presided over the endless battle of Hjadningavig. This was similar to the fights outside Valhol, except that it was a clash between two mortal armies maintained eternally by bringing the casualties back to life each night. It is said to take place on an island that was identified by Snorri Sturluson as being in the Orkneys.

The halls of Valhol and Folkvangr were open only to the best of those who died in battle. Those who died at sea went to the realm of Ran, and everyone else was the concern of Hel. The idea of Helheim as being a grim underworld is likely a Christian distortion; the word Hel itself originally had connotations of concealment or hiding rather than death, perhaps suggesting that the dead passed beyond the perception of mortals.

Helheim, realm of Hel, is described as lying under a root of Yggdrasil in Niflheim surrounded by a wall of high mountains, and is entered by crossing the bridge Gjallarbru over the river Gjoll, then passing through a great gate that does not allow the dead back out again.

The fate of the dead who did not qualify for entry to Valhol or Folkvang seems to vary

## WHAT IS VALHOL?

Valhol, which translates as 'hall of the slain', is often called Valhalla, but this is in fact a fairly modern corruption of the name. It was located in Odin's realm of Gladsheim, and was a very martial place with spear-shafts for rafters and a roof made of shields, but it is described as rising peacefully when first sighted as someone approached. In front of Valhol was the gate Valgrind, and the hall itself had 540 doors, so that fully 800 warriors could come out at once. Thor's hall Bilskirnir is said to be within Valhol, although other references say it is in Thrudvang ('Field of Strength'). Either way, Odin refers to Bilskirnir's 540 rooms as making it the largest hall within Valhol.

LEFT: **This pre-Viking Age figurine probably depicts Freyja. Despite being a fertility goddess she presided over Folkvangr, which seems to have been a place very similar to Odin's Valhol.**

according to the source. In old Norse mythology there was no definite equivalent to the monotheistic 'heaven for the good and hell for the bad' concept. Some of the people who entered the realm of Hel are noted as being punished for their deeds in life. Typically they were adulterers, kin-slayers and oath-breakers – the three often went together in Norse society – who were considered the worst of criminals.

Crimes such as kin-slaying and oath-breaking were not merely bad for society, they were considered to bring closer the onset of Ragnarok. This makes the killing of Baldr especially reprehensible, and also accounts for the many times that an enraged Thor stopped short of slaying Loki, adopted brother of his father. Those that committed these crimes were doomed to spend eternity in Nastrond, the corpse-shore, where the dragon Nidhogg nibbled on their corpses and sucked out their blood.

Most people seem to have had a generally happier existence in the realm of Hel. There are references to the dead having a fairly normal existence – if that is the right word – after death, doing the same sort of things that they did during their mortal life. In the western Norse regions, such as Iceland, the idea became prevalent of a holy mountain named Helgafjell where the dead spent their time drinking and talking around a warm hearth.

Helgafjell was reported by seers as being a peaceful, comfortable place not very different to being alive on Earth.

There are also references to how the unrighteous would be condemned to a place called Niflhel ('Misty Hel'), and that the righteous would go to Gimle (also called Sintri, depending on the source). The implication is that Gimle is a sort of heaven located in Asgard, but Gimle is also stated to be the home of the survivors after Ragnarok. It may be that this means the dead can hope to be resurrected in the new world after Ragnarok, but this whole concept seems to be rife with Christian influences and may be a distortion of the original version.

The tale of the slaying of Baldr offers many insights into the process of death and the afterlife; it also presents some intriguing implications. Although Baldr died of violence, this was a rather foolish game and not a glorious battle. He was essentially a murder victim rather than a warrior facing his foes. Thus presumably Baldr did not qualify for entry to Valhol or Folkvang. Odin never had any problem bending or completely ignoring the laws of men

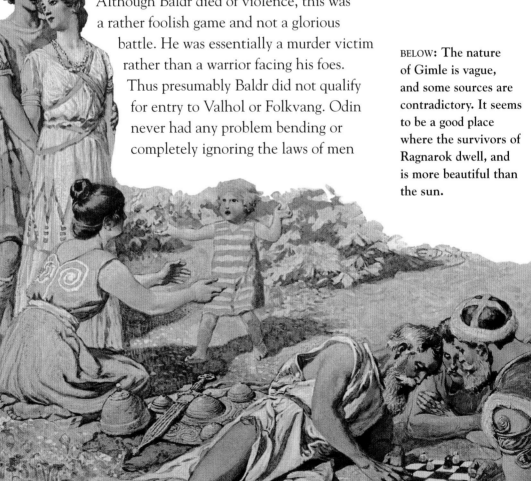

BELOW: The nature of Gimle is vague, and some sources are contradictory. It seems to be a good place where the survivors of Ragnarok dwell, and is more beautiful than the sun.

and gods, yet there is no mention of an attempt to make a special dispensation for Baldr, suggesting that the laws of death are beyond even mighty Odin's capabilities to circumvent. It was prophesied that Baldr would return after Ragnarok in the new age of wonder and glory, but until then he was as dead as anyone else and must remain in Hel's realm.

## Funeral Rites

The process of getting from the world of the living to whatever afterlife awaited a given individual was complex, and beliefs may have varied from place to place or over time. It appears that the Norse religion considered a person's essence of being to be composed of several parts. The Hamingja was a part of the person's spirit that could be passed to a descendant. The word translates roughly as 'luck', suggesting that a dead ancestor's fortunes might influence the life of another family member.

Worship of ancestors was not uncommon, and a particularly nasty ancestor might haunt and trouble his descendants. There is much confusion between venerated ancestors and Elves, and indeed the two might be more or less the same thing. Elves were powerful supernatural beings; so were some ancestors. Norse religion was not especially precise in its terminology, so perhaps a notable ancestor 'became' an Elf – either literally by some form of transformation or by being referred to as one to denote his new status.

CROWS AND WOLVES DESTROYED THE BODIES OF THE SLAIN AND FREED THEIR SOULS TO BE TAKEN TO VALHOL OR FOLKVANG.

Another part of the person's essence, or soul, went on to whichever afterlife awaited him. There is evidence that this process was dependent on the destruction of the mortal body. This is one reason why Valkyries were associated with carrion creatures such as crows, or were at times said to take the form of such creatures. Crows, wolves and other animals destroyed the bodies of the slain and thus freed their souls to be taken to Valhol or Folkvang.

For those who did not die in battle, funeral rites varied. Burial was not uncommon, in which case the destruction of the body would take a lot longer than if cremation occurred. However,

LEFT: Ships feature
prominently in Viking
and pre-Viking funeral
rites. Some were set
adrift and burned, some
buried and some burned
and then buried. The
ship may have acted as a
spiritual vehicle to take
the dead to the afterlife.

a week after death a funeral feast was held. This was named
Sjaund, and at it a funeral ale with the same name was drunk.
Once this social ritual had been completed the person was
assumed to be truly dead and his heirs could inherit his goods or
status as the head of a household.

Not all of the dead stayed that way, and for this reason it was
not uncommon for slaves to be buried with their dead master
or for thralls to be given a simple grave to prevent them from
wandering around after death. The means were often simple:
pinning or stitching the feet together or binding limbs. Mystical
methods included burying certain objects with the body, or
taking a confusing route to the gravesite so that the dead person
inside the coffin would be disorientated and unable to return. A
'corpse door' over a burial mound was another effective barrier,
trapping the unquiet dead inside, since they could not leave
except by the proper entrance.

OPPOSITE: Grave-goods are common in many cultures. For the dead, they are useful items taken into the afterlife; for the living, a way of honouring a well-respected family member or friend.

BELOW: The Viking funeral has become a popular image in our culture, but probably did not occur very often. Building a ship was an expensive undertaking; destroying one would only make sense if it honoured a very powerful or rich person.

Those who did return from beyond the grave were named 'draug', and could be given a second death by the destruction of their bodies or removal of their heads. Until this happened draug could often perform magic. This ranged from the ability to enter dreams to shapeshifting, or moving through the ground by mystical means. Draug were normally the result of a malevolent person returning to their body to cause more trouble, but they could also be created if a person were killed by another draug. Some draug were able to wander freely. Those that were not and were thus restricted to their burial mound or the area close to it were named 'hangbui'.

Destruction of the body not only prevented it from becoming a 'draug' but also facilitated the passage to the afterlife. Cremation ensured this, but the Viking funeral portrayed in popular culture was by no means prevalent. The tale of Baldr includes the archetype of the ship-cremation, in which Baldr's wife (who had died of grief) and an unfortunate passing Dwarf (who had been kicked by Thor, but was presumably still alive) were burned with him. There are also references to the trimming

of a corpse's nails in order to prevent a different sort of return. At Ragnarok, the ship *Naglfari* (made from the nails of the dead) would convey the enemy to Asgard. Trimming a corpse's nails was said to delay the construction of the vessel.

Ships featured in many Norse funerals, not all of them at sea. Stone ships were used as burial chambers for important people, and wooden ships were sometimes buried rather than being set adrift and burned. Many archaeological finds have been made from ship-burial sites, with the grave-goods telling us much about the Norse way of life.

## Norse Funerals

There are few surviving accounts of Norse funerals. Of these, that written by the Arab scholar Ahmad ibn Fadlan is the most well known. He witnessed the funeral of a chieftain or prince who had died while on an expedition down the river Volga. The chieftain was temporarily interred while preparations were made, then placed in his bed in a longship brought ashore for the purpose. His grave-goods included fine clothing, food and drink, and animals including two horses, as well as his weapons.

The rites included an orgiastic element probably connected with sending the chieftain's life force into the next world. A female thrall, apparently a volunteer, was given strong drink until she entered an ecstatic state and had ritual sex with several men. She was then killed by an elderly woman (presumably a priestess) while restrained by the same men. The ship was then burned and a mound raised over the remains. Afterwards the Norsemen

## BURIED TREASURES

Grave-goods were common in Norse burials at all social levels. A craftsman might have tools, a noble would have precious items, and most free people had weapons. Weapons were also buried with women at times, and there is much discussion about how often this occurred. It is not currently known how common female warriors were, and whether the burial of a sword with a woman meant that she was actually a fighter. Indeed, for many years unearthed bodies were simply assumed to be male if they had weapons. New evidence may indicate that female warriors were more common than previously thought … or not. Time will tell.

ABOVE: The events of Ragnarok are depicted in many stone carvings. Here Odin, with a raven on his shoulder, is being eaten by the wolf Fenrir as was prophesied.

departed, and it is quite possible that the place had no special significance thereafter, since their chieftain had gone to the other world.

## Death and Renewal

The Norse religion was fateful and cyclic – everything died, but death was not the end of the cycle. Ragnarok was thus a time of great destruction, but also a chance for renewal. It was inevitable, creeping ever closer as certain events unfolded, but it was possible to delay or at least not hasten the end. Kin-slaying and oath-breaking – and not trimming the nails of corpses – could hasten Ragnarok, and at one point the giant Hymir feared that Thor was about to trigger the final battle by slaying Jormungand prematurely. Unlike most of the tales, which relate to events that have already happened, Ragnarok is a prophecy of what is to come.

*Gotterdammerung*, or 'Twilight of the Gods', comes from the Germanic versions of the same tale. The meaning is more or less the same, although there has been much scholarly debate about interpretation and linguistic links. Whichever term is used can be taken to refer to the doom of the gods, although 'doom' does not necessarily mean disaster. The term can more usefully be taken to mean 'fate' – Ragnarok was destined to occur from the moment Odin slew Ymir, and possibly before. However, in keeping with the Norse belief that fate is at least slightly malleable, the gods were doomed to fight at Ragnarok, although they did have some influence over the outcome.

The beginning of Ragnarok is signified by three winters of war in Midgard followed by the onset of Fimbulvetr. This is three years of winter with no respite and is a thoroughly unpleasant time on Earth, described as a sword age, an axe age, a wind age or a wolf age in which kin slay one another, society breaks down and none have mercy even upon former friends. This is the result of the wolves Hati and Skoll finally catching the sun and moon. Skoll swallows the sun and Hati mauls the moon. The stars go out and the Earth trembles, causing many things once bound to break free.

**AT RAGNAROK THE GODS WILL FACE TWO ARMIES OF GIANTS, A HORDE OF THE DEAD AND ASSORTED MONSTROUS OFFSPRING OF LOKI.**

The beginning of Ragnarok proper is signified by the crowing of three roosters – one in Asgard, one in Jotunheim and one in Helheim. Heimdall blows his horn Gjallarhorn to warn the gods, and the Midgard serpent Jormungand approaches the land, sending great destructive waves ashore. These also cause the corpse-nail ship *Naglfar* to break free from its moorings.

Loki and Fenrir are also freed. Loki brings an army from Hel (presumably the kinslayers and adulterers from Nastrond) and the army of giants sails in the ship *Naglfar*. Some sources have Loki as captain of this ship, some the giant Hrym. *Naglfar* is the largest ship in the world, and can hold a horde of giants.

LEFT: The fire giant Surt sets Asgard on fire with his flaming sword, and ultimately the flames burn and destroy the whole world. This is necessary if it is to be renewed.

Another army of Jotnar marches from Muspelheim behind the fire giant Surt.

After taking counsel with the other gods and at the Well of Mimir, Odin leads the gods and Einherjar out to the plain of Vigrid. As Surt sets the world afire with his blazing sword, many of the gods encounter ancient foes and battle to mutual destruction. Odin is swallowed by the wolf Fenrir, and is then avenged by his son Vidar, who forces the wolf's jaws apart with his feet and plunges a spear into his heart. Thor slays Jormungand, but is poisoned by the serpent's venom. He manages to walk nine steps before dying.

Freyr confronts the giant Surt, but has no sword, since he loaned his own to his servant Skirnir. He is slain by Surt but manages to stab him in the eye in some versions of the tale. Meanwhile, faithful Heimdall and trickster Loki meet in combat, slaying one another. Tyr, who lost his hand to Fenrir, battles the great hound Garm; both slay one another. Hel marches against Asgard with a legion of the dead, but Baldr and his brother Hod return from Helheim and fight on the side of the gods.

Surt's fire destroys everything – Asgard and Midgard are burned, as is Jotunheim and even icy Niflheim. The wreckage sinks into the ocean as the dragon Nidhogg flies over the battlefield looking for corpses to devour. When the battle is over, it seems that everything is dead and the world is broken.

ABOVE: Baldr is able to leave or escape from the realm of Hel and join the gods for their final battle. He survives the destruction of the cosmos, bringing his beauty and majesty into the new world.

RIGHT: The post-Ragnarok cosmos is fresh, new and wonderful. It is not completely beautiful and friendly, but the survivors are at least given the chance to start over and build a new world.

Then the land rises up again out of the sea, renewed with crops already growing in fields that do not need sowing. A new and even more beautiful sun shines down, and two humans have survived, sheltered in the world tree Yggdrasil. The surviving gods go to Idavoll, where Asgard used to be. Among them are Magni and Modi, Thor's heirs and now the owners of Mjolnir. Odin's sons Vidar and Vali make their way there, too, along with Hoenir. Hod and Baldr also survive.

The warriors of Valhol and Folkvang who survived the battle win themselves a place in the new world, which is better than the old one even before strife and malice damaged it. They have a hall named Gimle in what used to be Asgard, and there are other good places, too. The hall of Brimir always has plenty to drink, and good and righteous people will dwell in the hall of Sindri. In this new world there is also a hall on the corpse-shore of Nastrond, whose walls are made of snakes that spit venom constantly. This is where oath-breakers must live, endlessly wading through rivers of serpent venom and harassed by the dragon Nidhogg.

Parts of this image of the post-Ragnarok world seem to show Christian influences. There is now essentially a heaven for good people and a hell for bad ones. It is quite possible that the original myths depicted a future after the renewal of the world that was more in keeping with the original worlds as described in the rest of Norse mythology. This, too, is part of a cycle, like many in the old Norse religion. Myths are changed as stories are retold, such that the version told in 800 AD might be quite different to that of 1200 AD or 2015 AD. Yet to those who hear these tales as they are now, it is as if their version is 'how it always was'.

## Germanic Neopaganism

In the time of Snorri Sturluson (1179–1241), interest in the old pagan religions was sufficiently hazardous for a scholar that he had to present his collection of Norse

## RAGNAROK AS CHRISTIAN METAPHOR

It is interesting to speculate on whether Ragnarok and the renewal of the world is somehow a metaphor for the replacement of the old Norse religion with Christianity. This is possible, but unlikely. More probably the myth of Ragnarok, like all others, has been the subject of the inevitable change and drift that occurs over time. There was a time when tales were told of Tyr being the leader of the Aesir. Later, Odin was the leader and always had been, because that was what was believed in that era. Today's version of Ragnarok might be rather different to that of a Norse world before the coming of Christianity. The truth of a myth is whatever you believe it to be, so arguably the modern version is every bit as valid as the ancient one – but it would be fascinating to find out what the people of the 'Viking Age' believed was to happen after Ragnarok.

ABOVE: **Proto-Norse images are found on many objects unearthed in northern Europe, indicating that there were close cultural similarities between the Germanic and Scandinavian peoples.**

BELOW: **This gold bactreate depicts Odin on horseback. It dates from around 500 AD and was made somewhere in the region of what is now northern Germany.**

poetry as folklore and distorted history. More recent times have seen a revival of interest in the field, to the point where there is a significant modern religion based upon traditional Germanic beliefs. Not all of this interest was healthy, however – the Nazis made extensive use of Norse and Norse-style runes in their symbology, and have forever tainted many symbols.

The Nazis made use of runes as symbols in a variety of applications, notably the identification of military units in the field. Thus many Nordic runes have the potential to be misidentified as 'Nazi symbols' when in fact they are nothing of the sort. Examples include the Tyr rune, which was associated with glory and leadership. This was used by the Nazis as a regimental symbol and also as a grave marker in place of the more usual cross. The double lightning bolt, symbol of the SS, was derived from the Sun rune of the Elder Futhark.

The most famous symbol stolen by the Nazis is, of course, the swastika. This is one of the most ancient of known symbols, having been found carved into stones and mammoth tusks in archaeological sites dating back to the Neolithic era. It is associated with good luck or positivity in several religions, and in Europe is often referred to as the sun-wheel. The swastika was adopted as the symbol of several political groups in post-World War I Germany, not all of them right-wing, and the victory of the Nazi Party in the power struggles that followed also allowed it to take control of this symbol.

Versions facing in both directions have traditionally been used, although eventually the Nazi Party standardized their swastika as facing to the right. The display of the symbol is now banned in several countries, except where it is used for traditional religious purposes. It is still a common good-luck symbol in Asia, which has caused several incidents where items bearing what the producers thought of as perfectly innocent and positive symbols were imported into Western countries where they had entirely different connotations.

Neopaganism has also suffered from a supposed connection with Nazism. It is true that some Nazis were interested in the old Norse and Germanic cultures, but there the connection ends. Indeed, neopaganism considerably predates any twentieth-century political movement. It is hard to find a specific starting point, but there are examples of groups in the nineteenth century practicing runic divination and magic.

## Neopagan Religion

Neopaganism is – fittingly perhaps – a large and complex subject with many variations on the basic idea of reviving the old pagan religions. Different groups use various names for their religion, including Odinism, Heathenry and Asatru. Attitudes also vary, from people who are not very religious, but like the imagery and the chance to be a bit different while belonging to a community, to devout worshippers of the old gods.

Neopaganism owes much to the romantic view of the old Norse and Germanic world that became prevalent in the nineteenth century, and it is not hard to see the attraction. The gods of neopaganism are big characters whose epic stories involve battling giants and fishing for monstrous serpents. There is no single version of the 'holy truth' such as that existing in the more mainstream religions, since neopaganism has reconstructed the Norse and Germanic myths in all of their confusing and sometimes bizarre glory.

Beliefs and symbols vary considerably, although the symbol of Thor's hammer Mjolnir is very common, even among groups with radically different approaches to their religion. Some groups practice Seidr, the magic used by Frigg and Odin, and in some cases use it for divination. Traditionally, Seidr was more about changing the future than foretelling it. Similarly, groups that practice runic divination may claim that this is traditional, but there is little evidence to show that the runes were used in this manner.

Today, neopaganism is a fairly small religion – or, more accurately perhaps, a group of religions with a common basis – but it seems to be growing in popularity. The appeal of the old Norse gods remains strong, it appears, and of course there are a great many other Norse influences running through our culture.

BELOW: **This ninth-century carved bucket handle depicts Thor and features four swastikas. The symbol had positive connotations for centuries before it was hijacked and essentially poisoned by the Nazis.**

7

# THE LEGACY OF THE NORSE RELIGION

The old Norse religion was supplanted by Christianity a thousand years ago, yet its effects are still being felt today. Western culture was enormously influenced by the values of the Norse religion, as well as its myths and legends; many of the traits seen as admirable in Norse society are still highly regarded.

While pillaging is no longer socially acceptable, the sense of daring that went with the Norse expeditions is just as valid today. Norsemen rowed their open boats across the wild North Atlantic to Iceland, Greenland and even North America. The courage required to sail out into the open ocean in the hope that there was land somewhere over the empty horizon is quite staggering.

OPPOSITE: **This depiction of a raid in Ireland shows a Norseman clutching his collection of loot even as he attacks the village priest.**

The nearest equivalent in modern times would be three men in a tiny capsule voyaging to the moon – and they at least knew it was there! We have the same respect and awe of pioneers today that the Norsemen had for their own Viking adventurers.

Prowess at fighting is likewise still widely respected. There are many who disapprove of violence in any form, but even among those there may be a grudging admiration for the tenacity and bravery of a war hero. A significant segment of our society holds great respect for those who serve in the military and other dangerous occupations, and also for those who engage in violent and dangerous sports. The competitor who steps into the ring for a boxing match, or the cage for a mixed martial arts (MMA) competition, wins the respect of many – win or lose – just for taking the risk and accepting the challenge.

In a wider context, skill at combat pervades other segments of our society. To players of 'online shooters' – competitive video games where the object is to 'kill' members of the opposing team – a player's kill/death ratio is an important measure of his skill. More kills than deaths is a sign of an above-average player; a high ratio wins respect from other gamers. Thus the warrior mentality exists even among people who would never dream of actually fighting with someone in person.

BELOW: The discovery of America by Leif Erikson was the culmination of several incredible voyages into the unknown. First Iceland, then Greenland was found, and then finally the shores of the North American continent.

## Norse Values

The values put forward by Odin still have their place in modern
society – most of them, at least. The Allfather's views on the
faithlessness of women, his frequent deceptions and the casual
violence he often engaged in are not really applicable to polite
society, but his rules for the treatment of guests and similar
advice remain relevant. Other Norse ideals such as the effective
partnership of a well-matched husband and wife, and the
prohibition on harming women and children can also be seen
today – although arguably these ideals exist in most societies.

This enormous influence is not really surprising. The
Norsemen spread out over a huge area that included Scandinavia,
Iceland, the British Isles, the coastal regions of northern Europe
and huge areas of what is now Russia. Their traders voyaged even
further, and their fighting men served in large numbers in the
armies of the Byzantine Empire. Small wonder, then, that their
values became widespread and their stories are known far from
their lands of origin.

ABOVE: **The Norse
parliament or Althing
in Iceland was the basis
of the world's first true
democracy, in which
all adult males were
permitted to speak
and vote on important
matters.**

The 'Vikings' did not disappear or suddenly cease to have any influence. Christianity replaced Norse paganism, but the stories of the old gods were remembered long after the Norsemen of northern France had become Normans and eventually kings of England. The Norse settlers who moved eastwards became part of the Slavic society around Kiev and similar areas, and were known as the 'Rus'. That word gradually evolved to give the name of a modern nation. The colonies in Greenland and North America are long gone, but Iceland became the world's first true democracy. The core principles of this early democratic system were quintessentially Norse – every man who was mentally and physically sound had a vote, and it was said that Iceland had no king but the law.

## Tolkien's Middle Earth

All societies evolve and change, and they do so constantly. So it was with the Norse way of life. It gradually evolved into something different, but could trace its roots back to the old ways – and perhaps therefore to the creation of the world by Odin and his brothers. The legacy of Norse mythology can be found throughout our own culture, often in quite surprising places. The most obvious, perhaps, is fantasy fiction influenced at least in part by the work of J.R.R. Tolkien.

Tolkien's greatest contribution to modern fantasy was creating the archetypical – some might say they have become stereotypical – 'fantasy races'. His version of Dwarfs as the hardy underground-living creators of magical treasures seems somehow familiar. In fact, Tolkien used the lists of Dwarf names from Norse mythology for his own creations, and he gave us one other legacy – the pluralization of Dwarf as Dwarves.

## Norse Influences and J.R.R. Tolkien

Tolkien was a student of old English, Germanic and Norse legends, and drew upon them heavily in the creation of his works. Some of Tolkien's fantasy tales are more or less retellings of Norse legends, and others use elements drawn from these old tales. A prime example is the riddling contest. In *The Hobbit*, Bilbo Baggins and Gollum engage in a contest of riddles, with Bilbo facing the prospect of being eaten if he loses. The way he wins the contest, by asking a question to which only he would know the answer – 'what have I got in my pocket?' – is reminiscent of Odin's all-but-cheating in one of his own lethal contests.

The correct word is 'Dwarf', and Tolkien himself was rather embarrassed about the error, since he was a student of languages. However, it stuck and is now as prevalent as the correct 'Dwarfs'.

Tolkien's Elves have also become archetypical. His work included different groups of Elves – some magical and almost godlike, others more primitive. Subsequent fantasy books, films and games have made Elves rather mundane, but the author can recall reading *The Lord of the Rings* at age ten or so and getting a distinct impression of Elves as magical and rather scary, at least in the early chapters where the main characters have no familiarity with them.

## MANY OF TOLKIEN'S CREATIONS HAVE BECOME ARCHETYPES THROUGHOUT MODERN FANTASY.

Tolkien used many of what are now the standard fantasy tropes, such as trolls that are turned to stone by sunlight. The gold-guarding dragon, Smaug, of *The Hobbit,* is an obvious parallel to Fafnir, although Smaug was never anything but a dragon. He guards a hoard within which is a gemstone that can make its owner go mad with greed – the ring Andvarinaut in gem form.

Tolkien also set out what would become the standard 'fantasy baddies' in the form of orcs and goblins. Orcs are revealed to be originally Elves who were twisted by the dark lord to make them both abhorrent to look upon and evil in nature – perhaps a parallel to the Light and Dark Elves of Norse mythology. Tolkien also included ogres and various forms of spirit in his work, as well as a plethora of magical swords, rings, armour and other items.

Tolkien's greatest creation is undoubtedly Gandalf, who bears a distinct physical resemblance to Odin. Indeed, 'Greybeard' is a pseudonym used by both Gandalf and Odin. Like Odin,

BELOW: The wizard Gandalf is an archetypical Odin figure, combining wisdom, swordsmanship and magic with a certain amount of cryptic deviousness. Like Odin, he disappears from the tale and reappears when the story needs him.

Gandalf wanders the world dispensing rather cryptic wisdom, and in the books at least, he is a mysterious and not always reassuring figure. The movies of *The Lord of the Rings* and *The Hobbit* mostly present Gandalf as a rather kindly, benevolent and friendly figure, a sort of fond uncle who shepherds some of the characters through dangerous events. The books, however, show a much more Odin-like side to Gandalf's character.

## LIKE ODIN, GANDALF JOURNEYS INTO DANGEROUS PLACES IN SEARCH OF WISDOM.

The Gandalf of the books is not welcome in some places as a result of previous meddling, and is treated with suspicion in others – not surprisingly, as he is a powerful and mysterious wanderer with his own agenda. While the Gandalf of the movies is powerful, the Gandalf of the books is dangerous and also unpredictable. He journeys, sometimes unwisely, into hazardous places seeking wisdom. In this he is exactly what Tolkien envisioned him to be – an 'Odinic wanderer'.

### Wandering Wizards

Other authors have used these tropes or tried to break away from them. The mage Ingold Inglorion in *The Darwath Trilogy* created by Barbara Hambly was inevitably compared to Gandalf by reviewers of her fantasy novels. Ingold is an older man, a wanderer and, like Gandalf, an excellent swordsman. This sort of comparison is unavoidable, not because Tolkien created the wandering old wizard first, but because the concept was already deep-rooted in our subconscious. Hambly's Ingold Inglorion is a sufficiently different character that comparisons are superficial at best, but they will always be made when anyone writes about a wizard who has even a vague resemblance to the Odinic archetype.

Dragons are a staple of fantasy fiction, and are usually the typical gold-guarding type. There are notable exceptions, however. In Simon R. Green's *Blue Moon Rising*, the hero rescues a princess from a dragon. She had been tied to a stake as a sacrifice by people who saw him flying by and feared he would attack them, and since he felt sorry for the poor girl he rescued her. She had made his life miserable ever since, and he is only

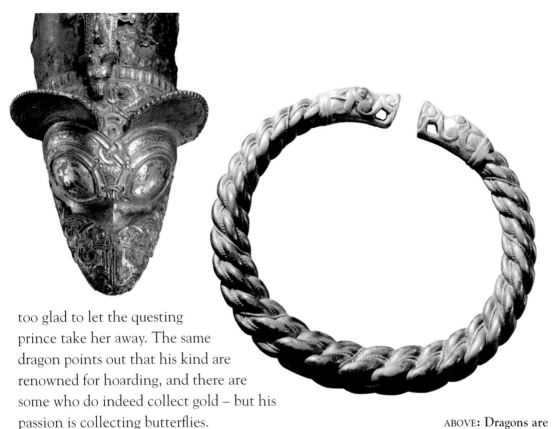

too glad to let the questing
prince take her away. The same
dragon points out that his kind are
renowned for hoarding, and there are
some who do indeed collect gold – but his
passion is collecting butterflies.

ABOVE: Dragons are
common in Norse
decorative items, which
are often highly complex
and extremely finely
made. The arm-ring
depicted here has dragon
heads as its ends.

   The dragons of Barbara Hambly's *Dragonsbane* are attracted
to gold, but this is because of its psychic resonance rather than
its monetary value. The character of Lord John Aversin, the
only man to kill a dragon and survive, tackles slaying with a
mix of pragmatic ruthlessness and regret. They are majestic and
beautiful creatures, he laments, but they kill people and devastate
the countryside. He also points out the utter stupidity of tackling
a dragon with a sword, preferring poisoned harpoons and an axe.

   Anne McCaffrey turned the idea of evil dragons on its head in
her *Dragonriders of Pern* series of novels. In these stories, dragons
are allied to humans, using their ability to fly and breathe fire
to defend human settlements from a threat that falls from the
sky. McCaffrey's dragons are of various colours, a theme used
extensively elsewhere in fantasy. Commonly, the powers of a
dragon and its general nature can be discerned from its colour.
The role-playing game 'Dungeons and Dragons' extensively
codified dragons (and many other standard fantasy creatures too)
into types based upon their colour. Those of metallic colours are

typically benevolent, while others are more likely to be typical destructive gold-hoarders.

The dragon of Mary Gentle's *Grunts* has a horde that is cursed, as so many seem to be. In this case, whatever you take from the dragon's lair, you become. A group of orc mercenaries loot a horde and find in it modern military equipment from our world, causing them to become, essentially, an orcish version of the US Marine Corps.

Orcs feature in many novels and games, usually as cannon fodder for the opposition. They are generally portrayed as brutish and dimwitted, happy to serve the strongest master they can find. Arguably, the Minions from the *Despicable Me* animated movies are a parody of this sort of callous, not-very-bright servant taken to a ridiculous and comedic extreme. However, not all fantasy portrays orcs in this manner.

## Video Game Tropes

'The Elder Scrolls' series of games treats orcs as 'just people too', along with humans, various sorts of elf and other non-human races. The orcs of this world are aggressive and bad-tempered for the most part, but they are barbarian people rather than generic 'bad guys with tusks'. 'The Elder Scrolls: Skyrim' is set in the land of the Nords, which is every bit as Norse in flavour as the name suggests. People swear by a being named Ysmir, among others, and visually the Nords have a distinct Norse feeling about them.

The main plot of the game revolves around dragons, thought to

BELOW: This tombstone in St Paul's Cathedral, London, is decorated with a relief depicting a dragon. Many carvings copy older styles of decoration which have now become traditional.

be extinct, but now returning to cause havoc. The dragons of Skyrim can fly, breathe fire and so forth, but do not seem to hoard gold. During the adventure, the player is frequently opposed by 'druagr', who are dead warriors roused form an unquiet grave. They bear a distinct similarity to the idea of dead warriors returning to fight alongside the Jotnar at Ragnarok. There are also giants in Skyrim, but they are simply very large beings who herd mammoths and prefer to be left alone.

The use of so many Norse tropes makes Skyrim feel familiar from the outset, and this familiarity provides a framework to hang a number of not-so-familiar elements on. This use of the familiar, usually elements from Western mythology that will be at least vaguely familiar to the player, reader or viewer, is a highly useful concept in world-building, i.e. creating an environment for a story to take place in. The use of the familiar means that less has to be explained or shown to the reader, enabling the author to get on with telling the story and presenting the unusual parts of his or her world in more detail.

FAMILIAR ELEMENTS OF WESTERN MYTHOLOGY ARE A USEFUL COMPONENT OF WORLD-BUILDING IN FICTION.

Similarly, references to familiar-sounding people and creatures can be found in J.K. Rowling's *Harry Potter* series. Norse gods turn up in Neil Gaiman's novels and even in Douglas Adams' *Hitchhikers' Guide To The Galaxy* novels. The advantage of using such familiar concepts is that they require little explanation and can also help a story feel more authentic – at least in some cases. This is not confined to characters and monsters; familiar concepts can be highly useful in world-building.

The world of Glorantha, originally created for the role-playing game 'RuneQuest', makes extensive use of concepts derived from Norse mythology, and lists the Eddas among the recommended further reading for interested players. Glorantha has barbarians who look remarkably Norse-like in many ways, including names and their attitude to oaths and kinslaying. Many of them worship an air god who can bring storms.

The deities of Glorantha are arrayed in several groups, some of which are inimical to others. They tend to be fairly complex

ABOVE: The 'Bound Devil on a cross' was found in Cumbria, England. Similarly, Loki is shown fettered after contriving Baldur's death.

entities, with unique motivations rather than a more straightforward 'good/evil' dichotomy. The gods of Glorantha are in many ways similar to Norse gods, each with one or more main functions, but all with a complex backstory that often involves conflict with other deities.

The current popularity of 'zombie survivor' fiction also has parallels with the 'draug' of Norse legend. In fact, it might be more accurate to refer to zombies as draug – they have more in common with the unquiet dead of old Scandinavia than the Caribbean version that they have their origins in. A common theme is that zombies can only be stopped by total destruction of the body or massive damage to the head. Someone killed by zombies will rise as one soon after. Both concepts are found in the Norse legends, although there it is a malevolent spirit that animates the dead rather than some kind of infection.

Some tales use direct parallels to characters from Norse mythology or events taken straight from the Eddas. David Drake's *Northworld* series of novels not only features characters who are science-fiction versions of Norse gods, but some events are paralleled in the books. Commander North (Odin) stirs up conflict to provide warriors for the final defence of the world, when the barriers of reality will collapse. Their souls, in effect, are collected by Valkyrie-like women, some of whom are captured by mortal men, or fall in love with them.

Other events parallel the Norse tales as well. A magical pendant is stolen by a trickster; a messenger threatens a woman until she agrees to marry one of the gods, and so on. All the events of the tales are leading up to a great battle at the end of the world, and North's need for warriors overwhelms (in his view at least) considerations of letting mortals live a peaceful and happy life. North has seen the future, and knows that he dies in the final battle. He does not know how events turn out after that and the battle is not depicted in the story. However, the reader is offered a shred of hope: North knows that at the moment of his death, the hero of the stories – a personification of justice named Hansen – is still fighting.

This rather bleak vision of Ragnarok is similar, in concept at least, to the many 'battle at the end of days' scenarios depicted in fantasy and science fiction. Some have no real parallel to the Ragnarok of the Norse tales, other than the dramatic use of the name. Sometimes the parallels are closer, however. The author's own *Armageddon 2089* series of novels deals with an apocalyptic future war that largely wrecks Earth. For those still alive when the fallout settles, a better world becomes possible.

## Movies, Comic Books and Popular Culture

Perhaps the most well-known adaptation of the Norse myths is the character Thor, who appears in *Marvel* comic books and movies derived from them. In *Marvel*'s universe, Thor is headstrong and often over-aggressive in his solution to problems,

BELOW: This depiction of Ragnarok captures the essence of the tales – there are giants hurling rocks, Odin leading the charge of the heroic gods whilst Thor bashes Jormungand with his hammer. Fenrir is ravening ... and overhead the sun is dying.

but somewhat smarter than the original version. His story is one of a brash and arrogant young man who learns at least a little wisdom, and he is portrayed as a valiant protector of both Earth and his home, the world of Asgard.

*Marvel*'s Thor is the son of Odin, who is less of a devious troublemaker than the original. Loki, in these tales, is the adopted son of Odin rather than his blood-brother, and thus the brother of Thor rather than his uncle. In the movies, Loki does not at first know that he is the child of giants, the enemies of the Asgardians. This discovery, along with his increasing resentment of what he sees as favouritism towards Thor, causes Loki to embark upon a plan to destroy Asgard.

In *Marvel*'s version of the Norse mythos, the Asgardians are advanced beings with godlike powers, but not gods as such. Their powers come from advanced technology rather than magic – although the two are indistinguishable to humans most of the time. *Marvel*'s Asgard has a Bifrost bridge guarded by Heimdall; its destruction by Thor to prevent disaster cuts off the usual means of travelling to Earth and other worlds for a time, although it is eventually rebuilt.

Odin appears in the TV series *Supernatural*, along with a being who claims to be Loki, but is, in fact, the angel Gabriel in disguise. Odin and his companions are former gods who, since their worship has been displaced, have become

BELOW: **In this depiction Bifrost is significantly more solid than the shimmering rainbow described in many tales. Legend has it that Bifrost will be shattered by the march of the Jotnar across it.**

little more than powerful supernatural beings. Odin mocks the beliefs of other religions, especially the idea that the world is balanced on a turtle's back, and states that he knows how he is to die – eaten by a giant wolf. He and his fellows are concerned about the coming 'Judeo-Christian apocalypse' however, presumably since the destruction of the world in this manner will also destroy beings from belief systems supplanted by Christianity or other modern religions.

There really is nothing unusual about creating a new version of a mythical character for the sake of a good story. Indeed, this almost certainly happened to the original tales, leading to the many versions that now exist. As noted elsewhere, the Norse legends themselves changed over time. Tyr was originally the leader of the gods, but later beliefs changed and it was Odin that was the leader – and always had been.

LEFT: Odin is depicted here in majesty, with his faithful ravens Hugin and Munin on his shoulders and his wolves Geri and Freki at his feet.

An example of this can be seen in *The Hobbit* trilogy of movies. Not only are characters such as Gandalf portrayed slightly differently – character development does not work the same way in a movie or TV series as it does in a book – but there are characters in the movies who are not in the book at all. The elf Legolas appears in *The Lord of the Rings*, but not in *The Hobbit*, and the female elf warrior Tamriel did not exist at all. These characters were added to *The Hobbit* movies to suit the needs of a screenplay telling the same general tale as the book, in the same way that a Jotunn might be invented, complete with backstory, to provide opposition for Thor or to be the source of some magical treasure. Snorri Sturluson, when he wrote the Eddas in medieval Iceland, is believed to have invented several details

LEFT: Beowulf is the classic martyr-hero, giving his life to protect those under his care. His battle with the dragon comes at the end of a long career doing great deeds and slaying monsters.

in an effort to make the Norse mythos fit together more tidily. That process continues today as new versions of tales derived from the Norse religion reach our pages and screens.

Other tales mix myth and pseudo-history to create a setting. Various versions of the tale of Beowulf have been written and filmed. The original is an Old English poem about a hero named Beowulf who aids Hrothgar, King of the Danes. Hrothgar's hall, named Heorot, is under attack from a monster called Grendel. Beowulf slays it, and then is forced to confront Grendel's mother as well. Many years later his own land is attacked by a dragon and he slays this, too, but dies from the poison in its bite.

The legend of Beowulf not only takes place partly in Denmark, but shows influences from the same heroic myths as the Norse legends. It has influenced tales ranging from straight retellings to more complex derivatives. In *The Legacy of Heorot*, a science-fiction novel by Niven, Pournelle and Barnes, colonists from Earth give familiar names to the features of their new world, and when a monstrous creature attacks them they name it the Grendel. Destroying it is a false victory; soon a horde of Grendels descend upon the colony and it falls upon a Beowulf-like character to save the colony. The story ends with an ominous statement that Beowulf slew the Grendel, but the dragon killed Beowulf, implying that the future of the colony is still in doubt. This proves to be true in the sequel, *Beowulf's Children*.

The novel *The Eaters of the Dead* (filmed as *The 13th Warrior*) by Michael Crichton combines the real experiences of an Arab scholar in the lands of the Norsemen with the tale of Beowulf. The eaters of the title are a tribe of primitive cannibals known as Wendol, who wear bearskins in a possible reference to berserkers of legend. The Wendol terrorize the local villages at night until a band of warriors finally have the courage to stand against them. The story also features a prince dying of a poisoned wound. It is notable that this story was written partly as a bet to prove that the allegedly outdated and rather dull tale of Beowulf could be made into an exciting modern action novel. This was a success, leading to a movie as well.

## Popular Culture

The Norse tales have also given us some semi-related pop culture. One of the most recognizable pieces of classical music is Richard Wagner's 'Ride of the Valkyries'. Famously used in the 1979 movie *Apocalypse Now*, it has become known (even among those who are unaware of its origins) as an excellent choice of dramatic soundtrack when doing something reckless or aggressive. The survivor group in the zombie-apocalypse TV series *Z Nation* play 'Ride of the Valkyries' from a speaker atop their truck while assaulting a compound filled with cannibals and the undead.

'Ride of the Valkyries' has been used in many similar circumstances, but it

# WAGNER'S RING CYCLE

The 'Ring Cycle' centres upon a magical ring similar to but not specifically named as Andvarinaut, which is lost to Wotan (Odin). He tries to regain it, sending the hero Siegfried to slay the dragon Fafner (Fafnir), but Siegfried is in turn betrayed and murdered. The Valkyrie Brunnhilde, sent to Earth as a mortal for disobeying Wotan, returns the ring to its original owners and then commits suicide. Finally, the gods are destroyed. This tale is derived mainly from the epic German poem *Das Nibelungenlied*, which is a parallel of the Volsung Saga found in the Poetic and Prose Eddas.

ABOVE: **A depiction of Brynhilde and Wotan from Wagner's 'Ring Cycle' of operas.**

OPPOSITE: Symbols
associated today with
the old Norse culture
include swords and
round shields, serpents
and dragons as well as
certain styles of art that
seem to just 'feel Norse'
even to those that do not
know their origins.

originally comes from Wagner's four-opera series *Der Ring Des Nibelungen*, more commonly known as the 'Ring Cycle'. This consists of four operas: *Das Rheingold*, *Die Walkure*, *Siegfried* and *Gotterdammerung* – 'The Rhinegold', 'The Valkyrie', 'Siegfried' and 'The Twilight of the Gods'. It features mortal and divine characters including several Norse gods (under their Germanic names), human heroes and Valkyries.

The secondary associations made by people hearing 'Ride of the Valkyries' can be taken as an indication of just how influential the Norse myths were on our culture. Music composed for an opera based on Norse and Germanic tales became so iconic that it has become almost a trope (or cliché, perhaps) in its own right. It is as if the original Norse tales were a big splash in a pond, creating secondary ripples as objects in the water were struck. No sign of that splash now remains, but the ripples have caused others, and those have caused yet more.

## CATTLE DIE, KINDRED DIE, EVERY MAN IS MORTAL; BUT I KNOW ONE THING THAT NEVER DIES, THE GLORY OF THE GREAT DEAD. – *HÁVAMÁL*

Among the wisdom put forward by Odin was the idea that everything fades away or dies except the judgement of a man's life. The Wordfame won by a person in life lives on – if not forever then certainly for longer than the lives of humans. It can be a way of transcending mortality – the things we do and say affect others, influencing them and through them, affecting yet others. Long after we are gone the ripples of our deeds spread out, ever smaller until they are lost among all the other ripples. Eventually they are lost to sight, but their effects remain, becoming a small part of the huge whole that is our culture.

So it is with the Norse legends. The old Norse gods have not been widely worshipped for centuries; the Norsemen no longer trade and raid around the coasts of Europe; the 'Viking Age' ended a thousand years ago … and yet the influence of this mighty culture can still be felt. Those who care to look can find the ripples running through our society even today. They are small now perhaps, but they are still there.

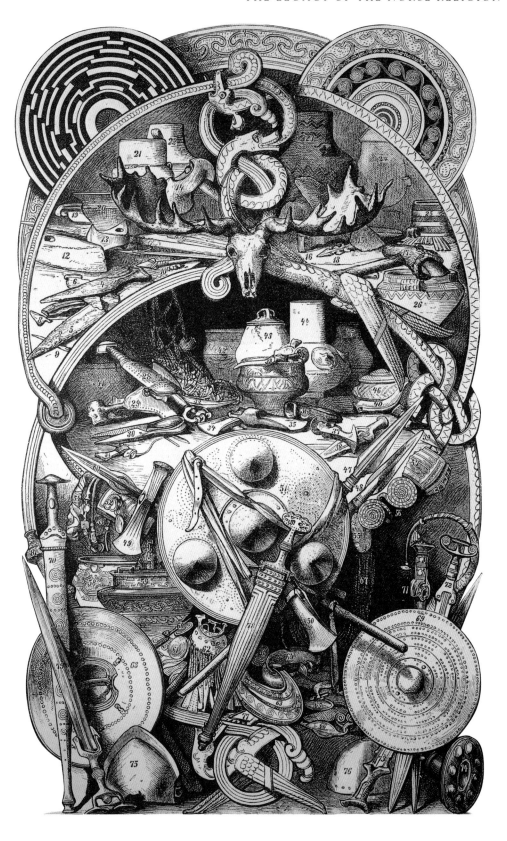

# INDEX

# PICTURE CREDITS

**AKG Images:** 35

**Alamy:** 8 (All Canada Photos), 11 (National Geographic), 53 (Scenics & Science), 69 (Image Broker), 77 (Mary Evans Picture Library), 95 (Interfoto), 121 (Imagebroker), 136 (Janzig), 149 (Interfoto), 160 (World History Archive), 167 (Art Archive), 171 (Imagebroker), 173 (Art Archive)180 (Interfoto), 181 (Historical Image Archive), 186 (Interfoto), 200 (National Geographic), 204 (Ben Molyneux), 205 (Pictorial Press), 214 (Mary Evans Picture Library), 217 (Historical Image Collection by Bildagentur-online)

**Alamy/Chronicle:** 30, 71, 73, 101, 113, 115, 126, 151, 154, 164, 195

**Alamy/ Heritage Image Partnership:** 14, 17, 26, 34, 41, 46, 48, 49, 52, 62, 64, 72, 85, 87, 89, 92, 123, 124 both, 130, 137, 138, 139, 153, 156, 158, 163, 166, 168, 173, 174, 179, 183, 187, 191, 194, 196t, 198 both, 199, 202, 207 both, 208, 210

**Alamy/ Ivy Close Images:** 30, 33t, 60, 67, 90, 97, 98b, 100, 102, 105, 107, 109, 110, 112, 116, 120, 125, 135, 142, 147, 169, 175, 177, 189, 196b, 213

**Bridgeman Art Library:** 33b (Arni Magnusson Institute), 80, 83 (Look & Learn), 98t (Look & Learn), 114, 132 (The Maas Gallery), 134 (Ken Welsh), 170 (De Agostini Picture Library/A. Dagli Orti), 172 (De Agostini Picture Library / A. Dagli Orti)

**Corbis:** 10 (Stefano Bianchetti), 122 (Stapleton Collection), 133 (Stapleton Collection)

**Depositphotos:** 12 (Doroshin), 20 (re_bekka), 68 (Zastavkin), 127 (Rudolf T), 128 (asafeliason), 129 (gornostaj), 148 (Kurt Hochrainer)

**Fotolia/Erica Guilane Nachez:** 54, 57, 59, 70, 104

**Getty Images:** 18 (Hulton), 21 (Universal Images Group), 51 (Hulton), 184 (De Agostini), 188 (Werner Forman Archive), 193 (Werner Forman Archive), 203 (William Gersham Collingwood), 215 (Print Collector)

**Mary Evans Picture Library:** 24, 28, 32, 42, 44 (Photo Researchers), 55 (Photoresearchers), 81 (Photo Researchers), 86, 93, 118, 212

**Mary Evans Picture Library/IBL Bildbyra:** 29, 39 61, 63, 141, 144

**Topfoto:** 94, 192 (Grainger), 211 (Charles Walker)

**Werner Forman Archive:** 6, 16 both, 22, 36/37, 74